299 Days: The Collapse

Book Two in the 299 Days Series

by

Glen Tate

Your Survival Library

www.PrepperPress.com

299 Days: The Collapse

ISBN 978-0615687469

Copyright © 2012 by Glen Tate

All rights reserved.

Printed in the United States of America.

Prepper Press Trade Paperback Edition: September 2012

Prepper Press is a division of Northern House Media, LLC

- To my real wife: I hope this book turns out to be fiction. I suspect it won't, but I'd love to be wrong. But in the meantime, I'm a man, and a man takes care of his family. I did. I will forever be proud of that, even if I wasn't understood at the time.

Book Two, *The Collapse*, picks up where *The Preparation* ends. Society begins to break down in this second book of the 299 Days series. The government stops functioning, guns and ammunition are in high demand, and a trip to the gas station has become more of a mission than an errand.

Grant and the Team know this is only the beginning, so they start taking steps to protect themselves and their loved ones. After a deadly incident in Grant's neighborhood, they being preparing to get out of dodge where they will soon learn whether the steps they took in *The Preparation* will be enough to survive the new reality.

The chaos and fear that begins to envelop the country will strip all the characters of what they know as normal. The will question what they stand for, what they will stand against, and, most importantly, who they will stand with.

For more about this series, free chapters, and to be notified about future releases, please visit **www.299days.com**.

About the Author:

Glen Tate has a front row seat to the corruption in government and writes the *299 Days* series from his first-hand observations of why a collapse is coming and predictions on how it will unfold. Much like the main character in the series, Grant Matson, the author grew up in a rural and remote part of Washington State. He is now a forty-something resident of Olympia, Washington, and is a very active prepper. "Glen" keeps his real identity a secret so he won't lose his job because, in his line of work, being a prepper and questioning the motives of the government is not appreciated.

- Book 2 -

Chapter 43

May Day

Grant had been so absorbed by Washington State's spiral into collapse that he did not pay much attention to the coinciding national collapse. The Federal Government was in the same shape as Washington State, and for the same reasons. He was so consumed by what was happening in Washington State, but managed to pick up on some of the major details surrounding the collapse across the nation.

The Federal Government ran out of money. Tax revenue was only paying about half of the money the Federal Government was spending each year. The Government had to borrow the other half. Interest on the debt was going up each year. Pretty soon, about half of the budget would go to paying off interest, which meant the government needed to borrow even more to pay the interest. Borrowing to pay for borrowing. The United States of America was in a financial death spiral. Anyone who paid attention could see this.

Most average Americans weren't paying attention; they knew the government was spending too much, but didn't really know the details. However, the foreign governments, especially China, who loaned the U.S. all the money, were paying attention. They knew that they were never going to get their money back. They had to cut their losses.

The second lowering of the U.S. bond rating a few months ago had been a shock to the financial system. Not a surprise, but still a shock. People in the financial markets had wondered why it took this long for the unsustainable debt of the U.S. to catch up with reality. For the first few days after the bond rating was lowered, no large holder of U.S. bonds wanted to be the first to sell off their bonds. That would lower the value of their remaining holdings. Small holders of U.S. bonds, like mutual funds and wealthy individuals, were selling, but the price wasn't dropping as fast as Grant had thought it would.

The bonds were basically shares of stock in the strength of the U.S. dollar, so when they went down, the value of the U.S. dollar went down. Slowly at first; inflation never occurs overnight. The government kept telling everyone that inflation wasn't going to go up, so people continued believing everything would be fine.

Then it happened. It was May Day. On that day, which was full of symbolism to the Communists, China started selling its U.S. bonds. The "May Day Dump," as it became known. Japan, Europe, and the Middle East followed in a mad dash to dump the dollar. The value of the U.S. dollar plummeted. U.S. bonds were being bought up by unknown investors, but everyone assumed it was the Federal Reserve buying through third parties. The Federal Reserve paid for these bonds with money it created electronically and sent to the U.S. Treasury. They paid for debt with fake money. That "money" could not be valuable anymore. People had lost faith in the value of the dollar. Dollars were only paper, so once the faith was gone, the value was gone.

Inflation started. It was not bad at first; but went up steadily. Interest rates went up substantially because the dollars loaned would be paid back in the future with dollars that were much less valuable now. The Federal Reserve had always tried to keep interest rates near zero to spur loans and spending. It couldn't keep rates artificially low, anymore. So, overnight, the Federal Reserve massively raised interest rates. Since the American economy ran on people buying things they couldn't afford with credit, when interest rates shot up, people really couldn't buy things.

The stock market crashed. Again. It had never really recovered from the first crash when the U.S. bond rating was lowered previously. Unemployment went through the roof; it hit 25% in about one week. America was in a full economic depression. Except, unlike the Great Depression of the 1930s, this depression had high inflation. It was the worst of both worlds: very little economic activity, but the necessities of life were costing more and more.

Separate regions of the country were affected differently. California and the Northeast had it the worst; they had the largest government per capita. This meant more dependency and the biggest shock and outcry when the government checks stopped. It also meant people were less self-sufficient. They owned fewer guns to protect themselves.

The Midwest was a mixed bag. Illinois was an absolute wreck. The big cities in the Midwest were like California and the Northeast, but the rural areas were doing better. Not great, but better.

Washington State fit the Midwest model. In the Seattle metro area, which included Olympia, government was huge and people were, for the most part, dependent.

However, in the rural areas of the state, which included Pierce Point where Grant's cabin was, things were better. People were less dependent on government, and a higher percentage of them were more self-sufficient. Gun ownership was high. Things still sucked there, but the situation wasn't as desperate as in the Seattle area.

Some states were faring much better. Texas and the Southern states, along with Arizona and the Mountain West, were doing better because they had semi-functional state and local governments. They had many self-sufficient people. Entrepreneurs and people who wanted to be free had left states like California and settled in those states.

Texas was still dealing with the Mexican refugee problem, though it was winding down. The drug lords had killed so many of each other that they were petering out. They were weak compared to what was left of the Mexican government. Some Mexicans were actually returning to Mexico because they found gangs and violence and starvation up in America.

It was still bad in Texas; Bill Owens would explain to Grant in their phone calls and texts, but they were getting it under control. Grant quit watching the news because the reporting was so biased that it wasn't worth watching. He got his news from Bill Owens.

Texas didn't have to enact any draconian measures like martial law. For the most part, neighbors were cooperating and the local police and the Texas State Guard was handling things well. The Texas Governor changed the name from the Texas "National" Guard to the Texas "State" Guard to emphasize its allegiance to the citizens of the state, not the Federal Government. People were fighting back against the Mexican and other gangs that surged at the beginning of the crisis. Arizona was in a similar situation.

California was a basket case. Gangs ran wild. White gangs, black gangs, Mexican gangs, Asian gangs. "Gang" was one of those words that had a different meaning pre-Collapse. Back then, it only meant a scary street gang, like Hells Angels or the Crips. While there was still plenty of that, after the Collapse, a "gang" didn't necessarily mean scary people. It meant a neighborhood banding together, cops who administered "street justice" to deserving bad guys, or a group of soldiers or cops who had been laid off and got together. Some "gangs" were even formed at office buildings among people who sat in cubicles together and needed to protect themselves.

While there were gangs, this did not mean that California or the rest of America started to resemble an apocalyptic wasteland. Many people were still living their normal lives.

People still took their kids to school and went to their jobs, if they still had them. Most people still had jobs as the unemployment rate was only 25%. People went to baseball and football games. They had friends over for BBQs. They did normal things, but the crime rate was very high and people were gravitating toward groups for mutual protection.

California police and the California National Guard, along with federal troops, were still under orders that they could not be seen as hurting minorities. It was a joke. Many innocent minorities were getting killed because there was no law and order. The California government got blamed for this, too. They couldn't win, because they weren't trying. They were muddling through. They were being bureaucratic, which is all they knew. They were following orders from idiot politicians. California was so racially and politically divided it couldn't function. And it was bankrupt. The state of California was ceasing to exist as a state. It was becoming a place on the map where the Federal Government was technically in power.

People began leaving California in droves. Many drove up Interstate 5 to Oregon and Washington. The California real estate market tanked with so many people leaving and so much violence.

The role of the Federal Government was strengthening in some regions and decreasing in others. In California, the Northeast, and the cities of the Midwest, the Feds were running things. The areas being run by the Federal Government became known as the "Former United States of America," or "FUSA." At first, the term "FUSA" was a joke to illustrate how the United States was not as united as it once was. But it was increasingly becoming real.

In the Southern and Mountain West states, which people started calling the "Southern States," the Federal Government was becoming increasingly less relevant. Many states, again led by Texas, were having their Congressmen and Senators take an oath of loyalty to their states, not the Federal Government. Some refused, but most took the oath. Southern States were passing laws nullifying federal laws. Oklahoma passed a law that guns made and sold in Oklahoma were no longer subject to federal firearm regulations. Southern states were passing laws reaffirming their Tenth Amendment rights, which was the part of the Constitution essentially saying that power not specifically

4

given to the Federal Government remains with the states and the people. The Federal Government was exercising all kinds of power not specifically given to it under the Constitution, like draconian environmental laws. Federal agencies like the EPA essentially stopped working in the Southern states. They had no money to enforce their regulations, so they just stopped coming to work.

The country was not headed into a second Civil War because it wasn't necessary. The Feds were so broke and powerless that the Southern states could just ignore them. There was nothing dramatic about it. These states, along with many Americans were quietly ignoring the Federal Government.

Before the Collapse, most anyone who imagined what dissolution of the United States would look like often jumped to dramatic conclusions. They would envision large federal and rebel armies fighting each other; like the Civil War.

It didn't happen that way. Real life is usually less dramatic than grand predictions. Instead, it was a gradual dissolution over the period of a few months based on the impracticality of the Federal Government continuing to govern, followed by the Southern states coming into fill the vacuum. There needed to be some level of government, especially honest police protection and infrastructure like roads and utilities, and the Southern states could do it. The Feds couldn't. It was that simple. It was practical, not dramatic.

During the Collapse, most people didn't want to choose sides; they just wanted the economy to be fixed and the crimes to stop. No one wanted the bloodshed that would come if the federal and Southern armies began fighting each other. There were ten thousand nuclear warheads out there, many of them on bases in the Southern states. The Feds kept strict control over the launch codes for them, but there were still ten thousand containers of highly radioactive materials that could be used to make "dirty bombs." Those were a conventional explosive that distributed uranium or plutonium in an area, making it radioactive. Not as big of a "bang" as a nuclear detonation, but devastating all the same. Very quickly into the Collapse, the Feds secured these weapons. They had planned for this.

There was another reason why there wasn't a fight between two giant armies. Oath Keepers and those loyal to the Federal Government were thoroughly mixed together; sometimes a unit was split down the middle between the two. Oath Keepers called themselves "Patriots," and those loyal to the Federal Government, "Loyalists." Each side knew a full-on fight with large armies, navies, and air forces would destroy both sides in about fifteen minutes. Fight over what? Who wanted to rule over the burned out and broken shell of the FUSA? It was like a couple that, instead of getting divorced, just starts doing their own thing but still live in the same house and go through the motions of being married. They still fight, but not the final showdown kind of fight.

"Don't Tread on Me" flags were everywhere, especially in the Southern states. The flags were even popping up in Washington State. There were quite a few Patriots in Grant's state.

The "Don't Tread on Me" flag, which was once a mild political statement, had now become a battle flag. It was a statement that a person had taken sides and that he or she were accepting the risks that came with that. Grant got a big "Don't Tread on Me" flag for the cabin. At the beginning, he didn't fly it out there because he didn't want to attract attention, but he knew that he would be flying it at some point. He knew it. It was that weird feeling of the present and the future happening at the same time.

Chapter 44

Quit Whining and Start Shining

(First week of May)

Everything happened so quickly in those first days of May. Each day after the May Day Dump of bonds brought some new amazing revelation that the whole system, held together with duct tape and chewing gum, was coming apart. The U.S. could no longer borrow money. There was a giant tax protest movement. Each day after the May Day Dump, millions of people were quietly deciding they would no longer pay their taxes. Arizona renamed its National Guard the State Guard and announced it would use state forces to enforce the border. Several states, led by Oklahoma, announced that they would no longer contribute to Social Security for state employees, and they would not assist federal authorities in tax collection or any other activity. Large communities in California were given orders to relocate because of all the violence. A gallon of milk was approaching $10. There were gasoline shortages.

Grant and Lisa were both home a few days after the May Day Dump. Grant was making some lunch when Lisa got a call from her boss. She couldn't believe what he was telling her. They didn't want her to come to work. She commuted from Olympia to Tacoma, a thirty-minute drive in normal conditions, but the interstate was jammed. It was taking two hours to get to Tacoma. Her boss also said that they couldn't guarantee her safety in the hospital, despite all the need for doctors as a result of the increased crime. The crime was causing the ER to overflow. People were running into the hospitals — some armed, some not — to steal pain killers. Lisa's hospital didn't have enough guards, and the ones they did have were unarmed because long ago the hospital decided it would be a "gun free zone." Doctors and nurses were being robbed in the parking lot and attacked for no reason.

"It'll be like Katrina," Lisa's boss said. "We're having the people who are already at work stay here. We're on lockdown. I wouldn't ask you to come up in all that traffic, with all the bad things happening on the roads, just to be in lockdown," he said.

Lockdown. Wow. This seemed so unexpected.

"Is there some way I can help?" Lisa asked.

"Maybe you can go in to your local ER," her boss said, "the one in Olympia, but I bet they're in a similar situation. Maybe a little less serious since Olympia is a smaller city than Tacoma."

"OK," Lisa said. "I'll see if I can do that." She then asked if her co-workers were safe. Some of them were at the hospital seemingly safe and the others had called in to say they would stay at home for a few days until this blew over.

Lisa said goodbye and wished them well. Just then, the doorbell rang and Grant answered it. It was Sherrie Spencer, their neighbor.

"There's been a break-in at the Kaczmareks' over on Whitman Drive," Sherrie said.

What? A home invasion in the Cedars? In their own neighborhood. One cul-de-sac down from his. He didn't really know the people whose house was broken into, but Lisa seemed to recognize the name.

"Were they hurt?" Lisa asked.

"No," said Sherrie. "They weren't home. It happened during the day. Can you believe that?"

Yes, Grant thought. This was no surprise to him, but Lisa couldn't believe it. Grant needed to find out more.

"I'm going over to see what's going on," Grant said. He walked over to Whitman Drive.

There were some other neighborhood people there asking the Kaczmareks the same questions. Grant vaguely recognized Mr. Kaczmarek from last Halloween's trick or treating. He was a retired guy.

"We were at work and, in broad daylight, someone just smashed the back door down, came in, and cleaned us out," Mr. Kaczmarek said. "Thank God we weren't home."

Grant decided to take a little social risk with the guy. "Do you have a way to defend yourself in case they come back?" he asked.

Kaczmarek looked at Grant like he had said something horribly inappropriate. "No," Kaczmarek said. "Like a gun? Why would I have a gun? They're dangerous."

OK. That's how this is going to go. These people are idiots. There's no hope for them. Just play along.

"Odds are that they won't come back," Grant said, changing the subject a little. "We'll keep an eye on things as best we can. If you

8

need anything, let me know." Grant said. If you need anything? You need a gun, you dumb shit. Grant didn't say it. He didn't want this guy to know that he had guns. Besides, he was done trying to tell people things like this. He had given up.

Later that day, another neighbor, who Grant recognized but didn't know her name, came to the door.

"We're having a neighborhood meeting this evening. It's about the break in at the Kaczmareks'," she said.

Grant thought a neighborhood meeting of the weenies, the term he used for all the progressives that lived in the Cedars, would be pure entertainment. He might as well go in case they tried to do something stupid that affected him.

"I'll be there," Grant said to the neighbor he still couldn't remember the name of. The meeting would be at her house. He was embarrassed to ask which house she lived in. She smiled politely, a little miffed that Grant didn't know his neighbors well enough to know where they lived. But she was running into that frequently in the door-knocking she was doing that day.

Grant told Lisa what had happened at the Kaz-something house and that he would be going to the neighborhood meeting.

"That's good," Lisa said. "We could probably use a crime watch here." Grant thought, oh, a crime watch with people who don't own guns. That ought to be effective. If someone breaks in, the crime watch can call 911 and wait an hour for a cop to maybe show up. Or just go online and report the crime. After it's occurred, of course.

Grant needed Lisa to view him as a resource on these things. Don't debate her, just try to reassure her, he told himself. "We should double our efforts on making sure things are locked," he said. "We do a good job, but I'll start checking the doors at night."

Lisa was relieved. Thank goodness Grant was being so practical talking about sensible things like locking doors instead of talking about guns.

When Lisa was downstairs, Grant went upstairs to their bedroom and checked his shotgun. He could quickly release the small luggage combination lock on it by keeping it one number off the combination. He did so in less than a second. The lock popped open and he unzipped the gun case. He had two five-round boxes of buckshot in the case. He wouldn't store his shotgun loaded unless things got really bad. He could load his Remington 870 blindfolded and instantly. He practiced often.

Grant saw his pistol case by the shotgun in the master bedroom closet. He kept his Glock in .40 in that case. It, too, had a small luggage combination lock set one number off for quick access. He opened the pistol case. His Glock was ready to go. He had a loaded magazine in the gun (but without a round chambered) and his small Surefire flashlight that went on the end of the gun. This way he could see what he's shooting if they happened to have an intruder in the middle of the night.

After checking that his home-defense weapons were in order, Grant went to the neighborhood meeting. He couldn't resist going there armed. He slipped his little 380 auto into his jeans pocket. There was no chance of the weenies seeing him carrying that, unlike if he had his full-sized Glock in a holster and his jacket got hung up on the gun and exposed it. He didn't want the weenies to catch him carrying a gun, which would cause them to think he was a whacko and then they wouldn't listen to his ideas about defending the neighborhood. But at least he had a gun of some sort. He was carrying them more frequently now.

Of course, Nancy Ringman took over as the leader of the neighborhood group. Grant hated looking at her. She was the one who had seized WAB's bank account. And now she was putting herself in charge of their neighborhood's security. Great.

Nancy was superficially nice to Grant. "Oh, hi, Grant," she said in her sarcastically sweet voice. "Nice to see you. We can't talk about, you know, the case."

No shit, we can't talk about the case, Grant thought. He wasn't here to talk about a case. He felt like leaving. He couldn't stand these people.

Nancy called the meeting to order. She was loving this. She was in charge, and everyone in the room needed her. Nancy had Ken Kaczmarek describe what happened. No one had seen a thing. The theory was that his place was targeted because it was near the exit from the subdivision. It had a fence around it so they could get in through the back, do their business, and drive right out. Then Nancy told everyone to lock their doors. No shit, Nancy.

Grant couldn't live with himself if he didn't state the obvious. He had to at least try to reason with these people. Maybe he'd get lucky. Maybe things had changed so much in the past week of mayhem that they would actually listen to a voice of reason. Grant raised his hand and Nancy called on him.

"The response times for 911 calls are over an hour now, if they can even respond at all, with all the cutbacks," Grant said. People were nodding. That was a good sign. "Maybe we should have some of us discretely carrying guns and driving around the neighborhood."

Gasps. Actual audible gasps. Oh great.

Not everyone gasped. Ron Spencer, Grant's Mormon neighbor, was nodding. So was that guy on the next cul-de-sac who was a retired Navy pilot. Len. That was his name, if Grant recalled correctly.

Silence. Nancy decided she needed to save this discussion from going horribly wrong. "Um, Grant, guns are very dangerous," she said in a condescending tone. "We don't want them going off in our neighborhood and hurting people."

Was she serious? Quite a few people nodded with her. Oh, God, these people were hopeless.

Grant felt a debate coming on, one he would surely lose with these people, but he opened his mouth, anyway.

"Nancy," Grant said as politely as possible, "I don't know how much experience you have with firearms, but they don't just go off by themselves. Those of us who are hunters carry guns all day out in the woods and nothing bad ever happens."

"Oh, so there aren't any hunting accidents?" she said, very sarcastically. More nodding of heads among the sheeple.

OK, this was a lost cause. Time to prevent too much attention to himself. He didn't need these idiots knowing he had guns, which they had probably figured out by now, anyway.

"You know, Nancy, you're right," Grant said. "It was a crazy idea. I'm here to listen to the neighborhood's solution. A consensus solution," he said, amazingly convincingly. "Consensus" was a code word he learned while working for government. It meant everyone would go along with whatever stupid idea the leader came up with.

That was it. He tried. He was out. He would defend his house. He saw Ron Spencer looking at him.

Duh, Grant thought. Forget the weenies. Just get some of the guys together who have guns and do your own secret patrols. You don't need permission from the collective to take care of yourself.

Grant sat through the excruciating chatter about who would be the "Block Watch Captain" and, for the umpteenth time, the instruction to lock your doors and cars. Grant wondered if the "Block Watch Captains" would get special hats. He seriously wondered if they would.

When the meeting broke up, Grant, Ron, and Len stepped out together. They found a place where no one would see them together... plotting. Plotting against the will of the collective to protect themselves from obvious dangers.

Grant introduced himself to Len, who said, "I'm Len Isaacson. I know Ron from Rotary." Good. That meant Len wasn't a government employee.

Ron started it off. "We need to go on some 'drives' during the night. Packing, of course. Do you guys have concealed carry pistols?"

Grant and Len nodded.

Great. Now Grant needed to stay up all night patrolling to protect the weenies. Grant was a sheepdog, and the sheep were really stupid. He sighed. That's what it's like during a collapse. Pulling guard duty and trying to save dumb shits from themselves.

Don't be selfish. Help others. This is the kind of thing you are supposed to be doing.

There was the outside thought again. Crystal clear. He hadn't heard it in a while. He started running the patrol schedule through his mind. They needed more guys.

"You guys know anyone else who will go on 'drives' with us?" Grant asked.

Ron said, "Yeah, there's a guy on Whitman, Dave Burton. He's a gun guy. Don't know why he wasn't here tonight."

Len thought. "Maybe Chris... what's his last name? Chris someone on my cul-de-sac. He strikes me as a gun guy. I'll check with him."

Grant felt stupid saying this, but, "Let's keep our 'drives' quiet. I don't need Nancy on my ass about this." He marveled at how screwed the situation was; he had to keep it secret that he as recruiting a neighborhood patrol to protect them. Most people would be thankful that a group of guys were stepping up to take care of a problem. But not these brainwashed sheeple morons.

Grant wanted out of this place. His mind flashed to all the security he had out the cabin, especially if the Team was out there. But it was too early to jump now. Lisa would never go for it.

Wait for things to get worse. You'll know when it's time to leave.

The outside thought was reassuring — to the extent something telling a person that things will get worse is ever reassuring. But it was.

"We're not just going to have one guy driving around, are we?" Len asked. "What good is that? That's not a patrol," Len said. He was right.

Grant had a set of Motorola walkie talkies. They were the cheap low-powered kind he had Manda take with her when she went on bike rides when she was little. They worked fine in the subdivision. Grant described the walkie talkies to Ron and Len.

"We could have one man driving around radio to another designated guy if there's trouble," Ron said. "If we have enough guys, we could have two cars patrolling linked with the radios. They could use their horns to signal the rest of us." A good plan.

"Since we'd be in cars," Grant said, "the weenies couldn't see our guns." Ron and Len knew exactly who Grant meant by the "weenies."

Grant continued, "We should carry pistols, concealed, so we have them at all times. But we could put a long gun in our car." Ron and Len nodded. Having a loaded rifle or shotgun in the car within reach was, of course, against the law in Washington State. Oh well. The whole point of this exercise was that there weren't enough cops around. The worst that would happen if they got caught is that the cop would seize their guns and car. That's better than not having enough firepower to repel a gang of punks. Besides, they hadn't seen a cop car within a mile of the neighborhood for weeks. The rules were changing. The old ways were going away. Grant, Ron, and Len were living the new reality.

"One-man patrols and a designated stationary guy, or, better yet, two cars patrolling," Len said. "With just three guys, that means we need to be patrolling or on backup two out of three nights," Len said. "I enjoy sleeping. We need more guys."

They agreed to try to come up with more guys. They would follow up with the two leads they had and try to come up with more.

"Hey, Ron," Grant said, "Could we meet at your place and organize things there? I'd have the meeting at my house, but I don't think my wife would understand why I'm out playing 'cops and robbers'."

"No problem," Ron said. "Sherri is cool with guns."

Grant knew that people needed deadlines and concrete things to do or none of this volunteer stuff would ever get done. "How about we meet back at Ron's house in a half hour and start planning." Ron and Len nodded.

Grant walked back to his house. Now, in addition to being a "survivalist," he had to hide being an armed neighborhood patroller from Lisa. Great. He had to keep secrets about the things he was doing to protect her. Why? Grant realized he was in a pissy, negative mood. He had been for about a month while he was helplessly watching his country being destroyed. He needed to get his head in this game. It was getting pretty serious. Quit whining and start shining. Hey, that rhymed. Pretty good little phrase, he thought. He smiled. Quit whining and start shining. That was his new plan.

Chapter 45

"You will be well taken care of."

(First week of May)

Grant walked into his house, still without having formulated a clear excuse for going over to Ron's in a half hour.

Lisa asked, "Hey, how did the neighborhood meeting go? Are they going to do anything?"

Of course not, Grant wanted to say. He would just tell her that everything was fine.

"Nope," Grant said. "They're not going to do anything." She looked surprised.

"So," Grant said, "Ron Spencer and Len Isaacson want to talk about getting some guys together and taking some drives around the neighborhood at night to keep an eye on things." He left out the part about the guns.

"I think that's a great idea," Lisa said. "What a relief that would be."

Wow. It worked.

"I think I'll do it," Grant said. "We'll have those radios we gave to Manda back when she rode her bike all the time. We'll be very safe."

"Good. Thanks for doing this," she said. Whoa. Lisa, while she was stuck in the current world of relying on 911, was not stupid. Far from it. She knew there were problems out there, but she couldn't come to grips that the solutions involved things like guns, bugging out to the cabin, and abandoning her home. Little things like a neighborhood watch seemed perfect to her. This allowed her very smart brain to acknowledge the problem of lurking criminals, but not have to come up with a "farfetched" solution like bugging out.

Grant kissed her. He had to try to get her to start thinking about bugging out. He knew this was risky, but these were risky times.

"Honey," Grant said, "I'm going to give the neighborhood patrols a solid try and hope that it works. I hope all this bad news stops. But if it doesn't, I have a very detailed plan so you will be well taken care of." He looked at her right in the eyes and said it again, slowly: "You will be well taken care of."

She had no idea what he was talking about. She will be "well taken care of?"

Grant continued, "You and I have an obligation to the kids and each other to be safe. That means we need to consider a plan to go out to the cabin, at least for a short period of time to let things calm down. I have… "

"No," Lisa said. "We're not going out to your cabin to live," she said. Your cabin? Wasn't it their cabin?

"No, no, no," she said, shaking her head. "All my stuff is here. All of Cole's stuff is here. We can't just go out there. Whenever we go on a trip, I always have to do all the packing."

That was because she wouldn't let Grant do it. It had to be done her way.

"We won't need to pack much because there is already a lot of stuff out there," Grant said. Then he realized that she had no idea how much stuff was actually out there. She'd never looked in the "spider shed" that had about nine months of food.

"No," she said, getting mad. "That cabin is your little place to go on the weekends. It's not a place to live for any period of time." She just stared at him. That was the end of the conversation.

Grant was insulted. All his work and planning and she was just going to dismiss it like that? Grant started getting really mad. He had to control it. He couldn't turn bugging out into an "I'm right, you're wrong" issue with her. He struggled for a few seconds to get control of his anger.

"OK," he said. "I hear what you're saying. I disagree, but hope you at least think about it. If things continue to go downhill and get dangerous, I will share my concerns with you." That was feminized speech he learned in government: "share my concerns with you." He had to talk to her like the normal suburban wife she was, instead of the survivalist he was.

He had to act like this was no big deal. "I'm going to get ready to go over to Ron's. Thanks for listening to my concerns," he said as he kissed her. She smiled. She thought she had won that argument. Grant knew there would be a Round II.

He got the radios and went upstairs to where he kept his Glock. He tested the flashlight on the end of the barrel. He checked the magazine; full of self-defense rounds, the good ones that cost a $1 a piece. He wrapped the pistol in a hand towel to get it past Lisa, and went out to the garage where his gun stuff was and got his pistol belt, holster, and extra magazines. He had his holster that allowed him to put his Glock in with the flashlight on the end. He quickly loaded the extra mags, put on the belt, holstered his gun, put a light jacket over it, and got a big Maglight flashlight. He had done all of this without getting caught by Lisa.

Grant popped his head from the garage into the house and said, "See you in a little while, honey. I'll be at the Spencer's."

"OK. Be safe," she said.

He went over to the Spencer's, two houses away. Len came by, about twenty minutes late. He came with four other guys.

"Sorry to be late," Len said. "Us Navy guys hate to be late, but I thought you'd be OK with why," he said motioning to the four new guys. Grant knew one of them, Dave Burton, because his daughter and Cole were in the same grade at school. The other three looked mildly familiar, but Grant wasn't sure they lived in the Cedars. After some introductions, he found out they did.

Grant explained about the radios. They decided to go out and test them. They did that for about an hour, trying from every corner of the subdivision. The radios worked well.

These guys were pretty decent. The new guys owned guns, but weren't hardcore "gun guys." That was OK; at least they had concealed pistols and permits to carry. They were the kind of first-time gun buyers Grant saw all day long at Capitol City Guns. He was actually surprised that out of the fifty or so houses in the Cedars that even seven guys had guns.

"We will have our pistols on us at all times, but will also have a long gun in the car," Grant said. "Technically, it's illegal but I'm doing it. Who's with me?" They all nodded. When all else fails to motivate guys, try shaming them into being a bad ass.

"I only have a pistol," said Chris, one of the new guys.

"Me too," said Mick, another of the guys.

Ron was a duck hunter. "You guys know how to run a pump shotgun?" They nodded. They had both hunted a little. "I'll set you up with one of my Remington Wingmasters. I've..." he caught himself, but decided to trust these guys, "... got a couple." He smiled.

Now that the two guys without long guns each had one, no one asked each other what kind of long gun they would use. While they were all on the same team, there was still something about not blabbing about all your guns. Each one said they had an adequate long gun in the car, which was all anyone needed to know. Grant realized that an hour ago these guys barely knew each other. They all were a little afraid about the government trying to take their guns away. So they didn't talk about them.

Grant knew what long gun he would use—his AR with the EO Tech red-dot sight. It made it possible to aim in the dark. It wasn't a night-vision scope. The target wasn't lit up, but the place where the bullet would go had a bright red dot and a red circle around it. The street lights would provide the light necessary for identifying the target, hopefully, but they would not provide enough light to use regular sights. Grant was very glad that he had night sights, whether the glow-in-the-dark dots on his iron sights or a red-dot sight, on each of his battle guns.

"Battle guns?" Did he just use that term in his head? Yep. It seemed to fit. This was serious shit.

They came up with a schedule to provide a two-car patrol from midnight to 5:00 a.m. It was May, so the sun rose at that hour. This meant patrolling every third or fourth night and having his weapons handy when he slept in case he heard a car horn. This would suck, but it had to be done.

For the first time in a while, Grant felt like he was doing something constructive out in the open. He prepped in secret and always knew he was doing something to deal with the problems that were coming, but he had never done them in public. Now he felt like he was publicly taking some actions to deal with the problems.

It was public because everyone in the neighborhood knew that they were out "driving." Most didn't know about the long guns; certainly not Grant's AR in the car. Nancy and the other weenies didn't say anything because they knew the patrols were necessary. People like her, the people who ran the government, had always had it both ways like this: they relied on armed and brave men to protect everyone, but they still got to be in charge and talk about how they hated violence and aggressive men. OK, say what you will, Grant thought, as long as my family is protected.

Over the next few days, patrolling was boring. Grant was getting used to the schedule. It was only every third or fourth night, so he could handle the loss of sleep. When he was on call, waiting for a car horn to blare, he had to be prepared to rush off to a gunfight. He had his pistol belt, with his pistol, in the trunk of his car, along with his AR. Lisa wouldn't look in the trunk. And if she did? So what. He was protecting his family.

Grant kept both guns loaded, but not racked with a round in the chamber. He always checked to see if a round was in the chamber before using a gun, so he wasn't concerned that he'd forget to rack a round.

Grant had a tactical vest, similar to those that soldiers and SWAT teams wore. He used it when he trained with the Team. However, he didn't want to be seen with it by the weenies. Grant would lose all credibility if he were caught in that tac vest. But he had it. He kept it in a suit bag in the garage so no one had a clue what was in it.

Instead of a tac vest, Grant used a small shoulder bag with extra AR and pistol mags. It looked totally normal to have one. He could jump in his car and be to most parts of the subdivision within a minute. He could also open his trunk, grab his AR and shoulder bag, and run to anything in his immediate area. It wasn't ideal, but it was better than calling 911 at this point in time.

Grant didn't just focus on the security of the neighborhood; he also had to worry about his house being broken into, which was his first priority. He kept his tactical shotgun under the bed. A few years prior, he had a shoe repair shop use their strong sewing machine to make a customized bandolier sling for the shotgun. The sling held twenty-five shotgun rounds. Grab and go. He wasn't locking it in the case. He knew Lisa would flip out, but he needed to have it ready to go if he heard glass break. He didn't load it, at least. He had practiced speed loading that shotgun so many times with the Team he could do it in his sleep.

Grant really wanted Lisa to know how to use that .38 with the laser dot. He asked Manda if she thought Lisa was ready to confront reality in this way. Manda brought it up and Lisa said hell no. Manda reported back to Grant.

"Well, Manda," Grant said, "you can train Mom on this in a minute or two, can't you?"

"Yep," Manda said. "But why wouldn't I use it? I mean, I know how to shoot and she doesn't."

Smart girl. "You're right," Grant said. "You will be responsible for home defense when I'm not here. Don't store this thing unlocked. Use the padlock set one number off so you can get it quick. Hide it in your room where your Mom won't find it."

"OK, Dad," she said.

Grant hated to sneak around Lisa like this, but he had to.

Chapter 46

Empty the Gun Store

(First week of May)

Grant headed off to work. No one was getting anything done, but the WAB guys were working hard on Rebel Radio. They put out a fabulous episode each week; there was a lot to talk about.

At WAB, Grant spent a good part of his day reading the latest news and talking on the phone or texting Pow, Bill Owens, Steve Briggs, and others. Pow was patrolling his neighborhood, Bill Owens was doing the same down in Texas, and Steve said things were relatively calm in Forks, but people were openly carrying pistols in town.

Not in Olympia, though. Life was going on as normal, which was really, really odd. Grant constantly wondered if he was overreacting. How could all these people in Olympia be so oblivious?

He would visit Capitol City Guns to quench his nervous curiosity about anything relating to the events that were unfolding. Capitol City was nearly cleaned out of handguns and shotguns. They still had quite a few ARs because the prices were so high; $3,000, or so. AKs were about $2,000. Ammo and magazines were through the roof, too. Grant was glad he had purchased his stuff long ago. And that he knew how to use it.

The WAB guys were still concerned in varying degrees, but didn't seem to be doing anything about it. One afternoon, Brian came up to Grant and said, "Hey, man, when the shit hits the fan, I'm coming to your place." He smiled nervously.

Grant didn't know what to say. He wanted to say, "No, you're not." But Brian was a good friend. Grant thought about it and said, "I'll do what I can but we all have to put our own families first." He didn't want to turn Brian away, but didn't want Brian to rely on him.

"Understandable," Brian said. He didn't seem to be as concerned as he was in the past. "I have decided to buy a gun. Would you help me pick one out?"

"Hell, yes," Grant said. This was more like it. Grant would be happy to help those who would help themselves.

"Tom and Ben are getting guns, too," Brian said. "Can we all go to the gun store? Like, soon?"

"Hell, yes," Grant repeated. Nice. These guys were taking some action.

An hour later, Grant took them to Capitol City and helped each one pick out a handgun. Chip managed to find some in stock for friends of Grant.

Ben pointed to a fifty-round box of ammunition and asked, "Should we get one?"

Fifty rounds won't get them through what's coming, Grant thought. He pointed to a thousand-round case of ammunition and said, "Actually, get one of those and split it."

They all got 9mm Sig Sauers, which was all that was left. They were fantastic guns, but more expensive than most, so they weren't sold out. At least Tom, Brian, and Ben could use each other's' magazines interchangeably.

Grant pulled Chip aside so the other customers wouldn't hear him, "Hey, Chip, could my friends get a case of 9mm?"

Chip smiled. "Yes. And, you're welcome." Grant knew how hard a case of 9mm was to come by. "But, since they're not you, they pay full price—$495. It'll be $650 tomorrow." Wow. Ammo prices were going crazy.

"Thank you, Chip," Grant said. He told the guys how lucky they were to have any ammo.

Grant took them out shooting right after buying their guns. He showed them how to take apart their guns and clean them. They were OK shots.

"We'll clean these now since we're all here," Grant said. "But if you need to use these, don't bother trying to clean them. They run just fine without cleaning them. I'd hate for you to lose a part and not be able to put them back together." Grant said. They were soaking it all in.

It was yet another amazing moment during a time that seemed to have several amazing moments every hour. There was Grant teaching Tom, Ben, and Brian how to shoot and clean pistols. This wasn't for fun. It was for real. Everyone sensed how much things had changed.

Chapter 47

Never Let a Good Crisis Go to Waste

(May 5)

Things continued to get worse. Congress had been passing laws like Washington State; authorizing checkpoints, more draconian civil forfeiture laws, and authorizing more warrantless searches. This was on top of a previous law, the 2011 National Defense Authorization Act that allowed the military to detain or kill anyone—without a trial— who committed a "belligerent act" against the U.S. It was up to the President to decide what a "belligerent act" was. No charges, no jury, no civilian judges, no appeal, no due process. At first, Grant thought the NDAA was a made up internet rumor. Then he read the law. It was real.

Even though things like the NDAA were on the books, America still wasn't yet under "martial law." It was not because the people running the government were such lovers of liberty that they wouldn't impose martial law; it was that they didn't have the ability to pull it off.

Thank God, literally, for the Oath Keepers. They had announced that Oath Keepers members would not carry out these new laws. That was the only thing preventing the government from taking over. The only thing. The politicians wanted martial law and most of the sheeple did, too. It was the "middlemen"—the Oath Keeper soldiers and cops—who got in between the politicians and the sheeple and prevented it from happening.

This was getting serious. Grant knew the Collapse was coming, and soon. The only question was when. The thing Grant was trying to figure out was when to bug out without overreacting, which meant bringing up the topic when conditions were clearly bad enough that Lisa would agree to go, but doing it soon enough that the roads would be safe enough to get out to the cabin.

One good thing out of Washington, D.C. was that they quit spending money. Finally. When it was too late. Now that they could not borrow money and were massively creating it, they decided to start cutting programs. In one stroke of the pen, they got rid of the annual cost-of-living increase for Social Security. That was a big deal with a real inflation rate of about 50%. They also capped Medicaid and Medicare payments to levels that no doctor could take, which effectively eliminated those programs. Grant figured Lisa would now start to care about politics.

Predictably, the tens of millions of people dependent on government programs came out of the woodwork. It only took a few hours for them to assemble. They protested like nothing the country had ever seen. Gigantic crowds surrounded federal and state office buildings in every major city. Since Olympia was the state capitol, it had massive protests.

Olympia and cities like it were overrun with pissed off people. The Baby Boomers were the angriest. They had been promised an easy retirement and free health care. What had happened? Who had taken it from them?

The protests in the other cities were getting ugly. Throwing bottles, breaking windows, riot police in every city, and clouds of tear gas. The vast majority of the protestors ran like scared children when the police showed up, but some stayed and fought it out. And lost. The police couldn't fit all the arrested protestors into the existing jails. They just gave them stern warnings and let them go, which only encouraged them to come back the next day and do it all over again. The system could not remotely handle this level of dissent.

The sheeple with their hands out weren't the only ones protesting. The Tea Party and some large tax protestor groups also rallied. They had put up with giant government for years and had finally had enough. They were not violent, although some radical elements of these groups tried to fight the police. And lost. Of course, the news showed the Tea Party arrests, but not many of the welfare protestors.

WAB's office was a few blocks from the state capitol. When the protests started, Tom told everyone to go home. The traffic jams were horrible. Tom pulled Grant, Ben, and Brian into his office.

"Given that WAB is a household name in this state with the libs, and how much they hate us," Tom said, "I expect some protestors to vandalize our office. I don't want our people here when that happens. Our insurance is paid up, so let's get people out of here."

Wow. Another amazing moment. Tom was getting ready for WAB's offices to get vandalized by a mob. This was really happening. Being a WAB staffer, and especially being on Rebel Radio, was a dangerous thing. Was Grant really thinking these thoughts? Oh, God.

The WAB guys were leaving the downtown Olympia area as the protestors were pouring in. They had seen plenty of protests before, but there was something much different about this one. There was an uncontrolled feeling to these protestors, like they were angrily screaming "it's finally happened." The protestors were meaner than ever before; furious, and egging each other on.

Grant got home early. Lisa, who hadn't been going into work after her boss told her not to even try, was out running errands. Unarmed. Grant was terrified for her. He had to put a stop to this driving around town when riots were about to start.

Manda was surprised to see Grant at 3:30 p.m. "What's up, Dad?" she asked.

"A bunch of dirtbags are protesting," Grant said.

"Oh." She paused. "Hey, Dad, when are we going to the cabin? This is getting scary."

That pierced Grant like a knife. "Yes, honey, it is getting scary. Do you think Mom will want to leave yet?"

"Nope," she said. "But I do." There was a long silence.

Cole came in and asked if he could have some pancakes for an after-school snack.

"Sure, lil' buddy," Grant said. How much longer would those pancakes be in the stores?

Thinking about the stores, Grant decided to venture out and go get some food for the cabin. He told Manda to take care of Cole, and have her .38 handy.

Grant headed to Cash n' Carry with his Glock 27. He wasn't the only one who had the same idea about stocking up while things were so crazy. The parking lot was full and shelves were getting bare. Everyone seemed a little nervous. Finally. People were finally getting it.

Some of the staples, like beans and rice, were already gone. There was still a lot of mashed potato mix, oatmeal, and pasta. Everyone in the store had a big cart full of food. Some had two carts and were trying to push them both along. People were guarding the food on their carts so no one would try to take it.

Grant got up to the cash register and the checker asked, "Have you heard about the bombing?"

Oh, no. It was starting. "Where? Here?" Grant asked.

"No," the checker said. "In D.C. A big one. Some federal building there. They still don't know what's going on." People around him started telling each other. This was what people were expecting, and news spread like wild fire.

Grant paid for his groceries with some of the last of the cash he had left in the expense-check envelope in his car.

Grant walked quickly out to his car and turned on the radio. A Senate office building had been bombed; there were lots of casualties. Not much else was known, except that the group claiming responsibility was called the "Red Brigades." The radio played audio from their website.

"Today, the Red Brigades took direct action to stop the dismantling of the social safety net millions of Americans depend on. We will not let corporations steal from you. Rise up. The time for revolution is now!"

Oh great, Grant thought. The tolerant, peace loving left was killing people. The media always talked about how the Tea Party inspired violence, but no one ever acted on it. Now the left had. The Right would get blamed for it, somehow.

Grant figured this Red Brigade group was probably a real one. If they were claiming to be left-wing terrorists, the government wouldn't be the ones behind the bombing in a "false flag" operation. That was the term for when a despotic government conducts or allows a terrorist strike and blames it on its opponents. If the "terrorists" had been Tea Party people, then Grant would have suspected it was a false flag event to get people to rally behind the government and hate the "teabaggers."

Grant saw some of the dead and wounded on TV. Even though he didn't like politicians, he did not wish them dead. He especially didn't like that now there would be a "crisis" that the feds would use to take even more power. Martial law hadn't been imposed, but this might be the trigger for it. What was it that a previous president's Chief of Staff said? "Never let a good crisis go to waste." The Feds would not let this golden opportunity go to waste.

Grant decided right then and there: if there is a crackdown, especially if people like WAB staff are targeted, then it would be time to bug out. Lisa had better come, or else.

Grant had patrol duty that night so he tried to take a nap. He couldn't sleep, so he just watched TV. There were more Red Brigade strikes. Chicago, LA, Miami. They were coordinated. No one had heard of this group before. How many more undetected groups were out there that would go on bombing sprees?

As Grant watched TV, the power went out. No; it couldn't be. Was some terrorist group taking down the power grid? Grant felt terrified for the first time since this had all started. He was terrified. He gathered the kids together. It was still light outside so he could see around the house.

The lights were off in the rest of the neighborhood. It wasn't just his house. Grant wanted to put on his pistol belt, which made no sense. A pistol wouldn't make the electricity come back on. And he didn't want to freak out the kids.

Grant just sat there with the kids. The house was totally silent, without the electrical gadgets emitting so much background noise. It was too quiet; terrifyingly quiet.

His mind was racing. He was thinking about all the things he needed to do to bug out. All the things to pack. How to tell—not ask, tell—Lisa they were going, and right now. Grant started to think about all the things that needed electricity. Everything. Life in America ends without electricity. No food storage, no gas pumps to fill up the semi-trucks, no medical equipment keeping people alive, no communications. Grant had planned for the things he could reasonably prep for; economic and political collapse. Those things could be handled with a cabin, stored food, guns, and a network of friends. But, no electricity? That was the one thing he could not prep for and expect a good outcome. Oh crap. He had prepped for everything except this.

Don't worry.

Then the power came on. Grant and the kids cheered out loud. Thank God.

The TV came back on, and in a minute or two was airing reports of temporary power outages on the West Coast and the Northeast.

That was weird. Grant thought a person who wanted to cripple or blackmail the United States would screw with their electrical grid. Was it just a coincidence? Shut up, Grant told himself. There were no more "coincidences" lately. Not on a day like today. Someone had either tried to take down the power grid and failed, or, worse yet, had the capability to turn it on and off at will. Oh God.

Don't overreact, Grant told himself.

Right about then, he heard the garage door open. It was Lisa. She came in and said, "The traffic lights weren't working. What a mess. But I'm home. How are you guys?"

"Mommy, the lights went out," said Cole. "We were scared but they came back on."

"No need to be scared, Cole," she said. "Everything is OK now."

Grant wanted to just be with his family at this time. He wanted to forget about the electricity, the Red Brigades, WAB vandalism, and crime patrols. He just wanted to be with his family.

However, at the same time, Grant had a burning desire to get the family out to the cabin right then. He fought that urge, although he knew that every second they waited, the harder it would be to get through the traffic. But, he had to ease Lisa into this. He couldn't be seen as overreacting even in the tiniest way.

"Let me cook you dinner," Grant said to Lisa. They had a great dinner together. It had been a while since they did. They were always so busy. They all really loved just having a nice meal together. Things were surprisingly good in that moment.

Grant was getting ready to bring up the subject of going to the cabin. He winked at Manda to signal that it was time for her to play along with what Grant was about to say.

Then his cell phone rang. It was Pow. This wasn't good.

"Yeah, man, what's up?" He asked Pow.

"Come down to Capitol City right now," Pow said. "Bring some heat. Discreet."

"Roger that," Grant said. Pow hung up. Grant assumed whatever he was going to do wouldn't take too long and then he could bring up bugging out to Lisa.

"Who was that?" Lisa asked.

"Ron," Grant said. "He needs me to go over to Len's. I'll be back as soon as I can."

"OK," Lisa said, "but try to be back to tuck in Cole. You know how he likes his dad to tuck him in every night."

"You bet," he said. "See you."

Grant went into the garage and hoped Lisa wouldn't follow him for some reason. He opened the trunk. It still had all that food from Cash n' Carry. His gun stuff was on top of that. He put on his pistol belt, with a light jacket over it. He left the shoulder bag of magazines and his AR in the trunk. Pow said "discreet."

Grant opened the garage door—yet another thing using electricity, he thought—and headed over to Ron's house in case Lisa was watching. After a minute in front of Ron's, Grant left for Capitol City Guns. He had no idea what he was heading into, but Pow needed him and he was very well armed. What could go wrong? He laughed.

The drive to Capitol City was a little weird. He did not see many cars on the road. He could hear sirens everywhere, especially off in the distance. Two police cars with sirens blazing were speeding toward the capitol, followed by a fire truck and ambulance.

The radio had news about massive protests and even small riots in San Francisco, Detroit, and Philadelphia. DC was a mess; it was totally paralyzed by protests and the bombing. Key government officials were being evacuated. There were lots of other amazing things that, in peace time, would have seemed like the biggest news of the decade. These included "lone wolf" terrorist attacks like mass shootings at airports and movie theaters, and the assassinations of various government officials and celebrities. Lately, however, they were just the latest headlines, soon to be outdone by the next hour's headlines.

As Grant got closer to Capitol City Guns, there was more activity. The parking lot was overflowing. The street going into the store was blocked. Pow's Hummer was there, as was Bobby's truck. Wes was directing traffic. He had a pistol on his belt. He saw Grant's car and motioned for him to come over.

"The store is closing and moving its inventory," Wes said. "Things are too hairy right now. Chip is worried that looters will come for the guns and ammo. We're putting up a discreet perimeter and getting customers out of here. Park over there and ask Pow what he needs you to do. You got a pistol on you?"

"Yep," Grant said and patted his right side where his Glock was.

"Good," Wes said. "No long guns should be visible. We don't need the cops here." Wes paused. "If there are any left."

Wes went back to directing traffic and telling people the store was closed. There was no time to chat.

Grant parked and did a press check of his pistol. Round in the chamber and the slide was back in battery. Ready to go. He had a full magazine in and four additional fifteen-round mags on his belt. Plus the AR and mags in the trunk. OK. It was time to help Chip.

Grant jogged from his car to the store with his hands out to his sides so no one would think he was a threat. Everyone was armed, except the customers who were getting turned away. Most were OK with the news that the store was closing, but some were getting pissed.

Pow saw Grant and said, "Get the customers out of the store and out of the parking lot."

Grant nodded. He was using his most polite voice with the customers. "Sorry, folks. The store is closed." Most were leaving. One guy wasn't.

"I have cash and want to buy a gun," the guy said. "Right

now." Grant sensed that the guy was a threat. He would try his voice first and then go to more drastic means.

"Time to go. Right now," he said in his strongest command voice which he developed after becoming a father and had to use it to get the kids' attention when they were about to do something stupid or dangerous. The guy stared at him, deciding what to do. Wait and see, Grant thought.

The guy just stood there; he did not comply with the order to leave. Time to ramp it up, Grant decided.

He moved his light jacket so his pistol was visible. In peacetime that would be the crime of "brandishing" a firearm. But this wasn't peacetime, anymore.

The guy looked at the pistol, and then at Grant. His eyes got big. Without saying a word, he backed away from the gun counter, turned around, and walked out. Grant followed him out and watched him get in his car and leave.

When Grant was outside in the parking lot, he listened to the sirens in the distance. It seemed like every cop and fire truck for a hundred miles was downtown at the capitol fighting the protestors.

The customers were out of the store. Bobby was getting them out of the parking lot. When the store was empty, Chip came out of the back room which was where the inventory was kept, secretly. Special Forces Ted was with him. Chip looked around. He saw Grant, the rest of the Team, and Ted. All trusted guys. He came over to them. He had a pistol on his belt, too; a 1911.

"Thanks for the help, guys," Chip said. "I need three or four of you to secure the parking lot. I will be bringing in my truck and Ted's. We each have U-Haul trailers on them. We have a little inventory to move out tonight. Like, all of it. The rest of you can help us move some heavy things into the trucks. Be discreet. Those in the parking lot can have rifles handy, but not slung over your shoulders."

Chip grabbed his gun inventory logs that ATF required him to maintain. He looked at them and laughed. "I guess I better have these in case things calm down and the law is enforced again." Chip shook his head, indicating that he doubted things would return to normal and those laws would ever be enforced again.

He looked at the guys. They were risking their lives to help him. "Thanks, gentlemen. Let's get to work."

Pow asked, "Who has an AR with them?" Grant, Scotty, and Bobby raised their hands. "OK, you guys make sure no one gets within a hundred yards of here. Be on the lookout for anyone who seems to be watching us. They might be casing the place. Tell customers we're closed. Cops can come here, but I'd rather they didn't. I'm not going to ask you to shoot a cop." Nice. This was for real.

Grant, Scotty, and Bobby went out to their vehicles to get their ARs and mag pouches.

Grant kept the safety on. He was pretty amped up, but he didn't want to hurt anyone by mistake. He went around to Scotty and Bobby. "Safeties on, guys?" They both nodded.

Grant used his car as cover. It was on the street and he had a good view of anyone coming the main way down the street and into the store. He could keep his AR on the car seat and remain discreet.

Bobby had his truck across the street from Grant and was doing the same. Scotty moved his truck to the other side of the store entrance, which faced a back street, so he could get anyone coming from the other direction into the store. Grant and Bobby had a perfect crossfire set up. That was interesting because neither one of them talked about where to position themselves; they just naturally set up in a crossfire. And they both had a good angle on Scotty's position to help him out.

Once they were set up, Grant was just watching. Everything. So were Bobby and Scotty.

Chip and Ted went out to their trucks with the U-Hauls, which were parked on the street a block away. They wheeled them into the parking lot which was finally empty. As soon as they pulled in, the door of the store came open and there were Wes and Pow with big plastic tubs. They looked like the tubs of parts Chip kept in the storage room. Grant focused on his job of watching the street to make sure no one came by.

After a few minutes, a car came down the back street toward Scotty. Grant figured that it could be a harmless guy or, because he was coming from the back street, it could be a decoy for an attack on the main entrance. Grant and Bobby grabbed their ARs out of their vehicles and got them ready. Scotty flagged down the car. He talked to the driver for a minute and then he turned around and left. Scotty flashed Grant and Bobby the thumbs up to show that everything was OK.

Wes, Pow, Ted, and Chip were loading Chip's U-Haul like mad men. Then Chip moved his truck a little and Ted moved his into the front of the store. They repeated the loading. They now had fewer plastic tubs and more rectangular cardboard boxes which held a rifle. Finally, lots of small rectangular boxes which held pistols. Then cases and cases of ammo. They looked pretty heavy.

An SUV came down Grant and Bobby's street. It was coming down Grant's side of the street, so Grant signaled that he would talk to the driver. He also signaled for Bobby to hide in his truck for surprise backup, if necessary.

The driver of the SUV could sense that things were a little unusual. The wailing sirens added to the surreal environment. Grant signaled with his left hand for the car to roll down its window. He kept his right hand on his pistol, which was partially showing. Grant figured the odds of being prosecuted for brandishing were pretty low when what's left of the police were busy fighting off protestors, and possibly rioters, three miles away at the capitol.

The driver rolled down his window. He didn't look fazed by the sight of a man with his hand on a holstered pistol. He was probably a gun guy who knew that Grant was not some amateur. Gun guys aren't usually scared of other gun guys. Someone with their hand on a pistol is not something unusual to them.

Grant used his confident, but not asshole, voice to say, "Where you headed?" He was trying to sound like a cop so the driver would assume he was and might listen more to what he told him to do. "Gun store," the guy said. He kept both hands on the steering wheel, yet another signal to Grant that the driver knew what he was doing; and knew how to avoid getting shot.

"It's closed," Grant said. "Try back tomorrow." Grant stared at the driver as if to say, "Seriously."

"OK. Thanks," the guy said. The driver paused and looked at Grant's exposed pistol. "Things hairy enough out here to need a pistol, huh?" He answered his own question by saying, "I guess so. Downtown near the capitol is a frickin' mess right now. That's why I wanted to come get a case of ammo."

"You and lots of others," Grant said. "That's why the store is closed for a while." Grant hated lying to people, but sometimes circumstances just called for it.

The driver nodded and said, "Have a good evening." He then looked at how he would get out of there. He said, "I'll turn around up there and come out the way I came in."

Grant nodded. He looked over to Bobby and motioned that the SUV would go up the street, turn around and then leave. Bobby understood, gave the thumbs up, and then gave the signal to Scotty, who gave a thumbs up. Hours and hours on the range using hand signals to communicate allowed them to do this effortlessly. Grant didn't want to give away the positions of his two colleagues, but he didn't want them to shoot this guy, either. When Grant got the thumbs up from Scotty, he turned back to the driver and said, "That ought to work. Have a good evening."

The driver did exactly what he said he would do. The turnaround was smooth and careful. On the way back out the main entrance, the driver waved at Grant. He waved back.

Grant was glad he didn't get shot or have to shoot anyone. Wow. This was for real.

He had a funny thought: How many other lawyers were doing this tonight? Actually, with all the protests and mayhem in the country, probably quite a few.

Chip came out of the parking lot and signaled that the trucks were loaded. He pointed to Bobby first, and then motioned for him to come into the store. He signaled for Scotty and Grant to stay put. Bobby walked into the store and came out a few minutes later. He signaled for Grant to go in next. Grant put his AR on the car seat, locked the door, and walked into the store.

Chip and Ted were inside with Wes and Pow standing guard at the door. The store was nearly empty except for accessories and cleaning supplies. There were a couple beater hunting rifles left on the wall, but no ARs or AKs. The glass pistol case was empty.

"OK, here's the plan," Chip said. "Me and Ted are going to go deposit this stuff in a safe place. A place none of you know about—no offense."

None taken.

Ted said, "Me and Chip can unload it by ourselves because we'll be in a much safer place and we don't want to keep you gentlemen here when we might have visitors."

That was appreciated. Besides, Grant had to get back home to start the process of convincing Lisa to go to the cabin.

"Thanks again, guys. Really appreciate it," Chip said. He shook Grant's hand and said, "Go tell Scotty to come in here so I can thank him in person. Then go home."

Grant shook Chip's hand. He shook Ted's, too. "No problem, guys. Happy to help."

Grant walked out quickly. This was not the time to chat. He motioned for Scotty to come in, and told him, "Chip needs to talk to you. I'll take your position until you come back out." Scotty nodded. "See you in a while," Grant said to him.

It was still quiet out by Scotty's truck. He came out of the store after a few minutes, and gave Grant the thumbs up, and Grant did the same. When Scotty got back to his truck, Grant said, "Keep your phone on."

"Yep," Scotty said. Grant walked back to his car. Bobby was gone by now. He turned around and drove home.

On the drive home, Grant started to wonder if he had just become an accessory to the illegal transfer of firearms. Yeah, probably. But the cops had other things on their plate right then. There weren't any cops around waiting to arrest him. Or so he thought. He saw red and blue flashing lights in his rearview mirror, and then heard a siren. Oh shit. The cop was right on him. Grant had a loaded AR in the passenger seat. Oh shit. He got very nervous; shaking-hands kind of nervous. He started pulling over. His life might pretty much be over right now.

Grant had a decision to make in the few seconds that it took to pull over. Would he shoot the cop? No, he quickly decided; he would go to jail. Then Grant realized there probably weren't any jails anymore, not for something like having a loaded gun in the car. He'd walk.

The cop car behind him sped past him, followed by a couple more. They must be going to the capitol. Thank God. Literally. He had been saying that a lot today.

Chapter 48

"Because this is my first gunfight."

(May 5)

By the time he arrived home, Grant had calmed down from his near encounter with the police. To say he was thankful to have made it back home alive and not arrested was an understatement.

He pulled off onto a side street by the entrance to the Cedars. It was dark and deserted. He transferred his AR from the passenger seat into the trunk. He didn't need Lisa or a cop seeing that. He took off his pistol belt and put that in the trunk, too. He noticed that here, near his neighborhood, the sirens were much quieter because it was a few miles farther from the capitol than the gun store. In fact, inside the houses in his neighborhood, he imagined his neighbors couldn't even hear the sirens. That might explain why most people in this area really didn't think much was going on.

Grant headed into his neighborhood. When he got near his house, he hit the garage door opener. What an evening. And it was only getting started.

"How was Len's?" Lisa asked when Grant walked in. Thank goodness she reminded him of the excuse he had used.

"Fine," Grant said. "We're fine tuning our patrol ideas. Are the kids OK?"

Lisa nodded. "Cole wants 'Dad to tuck,'" she said, referring to Cole's word for tucking in.

"Will do," Grant said. "It's the best part of my day. Are you OK?"

"Yeah," Lisa said. "Why?"

"There's a lot of scary stuff going on," Grant said, "and I want to make sure you're OK. I love you, Lisa."

"Love you too, hon," she said with a smile. "Yeah, I'm fine. I think the neighborhood patrol and police probably have this temporary situation under control, don't you?" She had heard the faint siren sounds and that made her nervous. She was fishing to get his real thoughts.

35

"Oh, yeah," Grant said, "I think things are fine. Hey, I should get tucking." He didn't want to tell her what he really thought. It would just be another argument.

Grant went upstairs and tucked in Cole. He loved that kid so much. He was so innocent. All he wanted in life was his dad to tuck him in. That's really all Grant wanted, too. But you can't have tucks when bad people are breaking down your door. So Grant would have to go out and keep the bad people away.

After tucking, Grant had to decide if this was the time to try to convince Lisa to go to the cabin. He wanted to get out there right away. Each hour that went by might mean it was too late to get out there safely.

Wait, the outside thought said.

OK, then. Grant would wait.

Grant remembered that his shift for the neighborhood patrol was starting at midnight, which was soon. He changed into his 5.11 pants and hillbilly slippers, went downstairs, kissed Lisa, and said, "It's my patrol shift now. Bye. Love you."

"Love you, too," she said. Grant sure was kind of emotional, she thought. Telling her he loved her so many times like… he didn't think he'd get a chance to tell her that ever again. It was a little frightening.

In the garage, Grant popped the trunk to double check he had everything he'd need. In the trunk was his pistol belt and pistol, along with his AR and shoulder mag bag. They were on top of the food in the trunk that he needed to unload later. He took the AR and mag bag from the trunk and put them on the passenger seat of his car. This way he would have them handy if he needed them on patrol. He put on his pistol belt. It felt so good on his hip. So reassuring.

Grant would be patrolling with Ron. Good. He trusted Ron's gun skills. That night on patrol, they talked over things, traded information about the Olympia protests, the bombings, and the power outage. Grant didn't talk about the inventory evacuation at the gun store, of course. His attention turned to the power outage.

"I don't want to freak you out, Ron," Grant said, "but if someone is able to crash the electrical grid periodically, things are… going to get rough." Grant was trying not to sound alarmist.

"Yep," Ron said. "Let's hope that's not it. Let's hope that some bird flew into a power line or something."

Grant didn't want to continue talking about simultaneous terrorist attacks and the power grid crashing. He would have said something that would alert Ron to Grant being a "survivalist." Grant decided to focus on the task at hand: a neighborhood patrol.

"We might go through quite a bit of gas driving all night, even at slow speeds," Grant said. "You got a full tank?"

"Yep," Ron said.

"Me, too," Grant said.

"Let's do it," Ron said with a smile.

They went to opposite ends of the subdivision and started going up and down each street and cul-de-sac. They could hear the sirens, but only faintly. They looked for anyone who didn't seem to belong. They were listening to the news on the radio. It was unbelievable all the things that were happening. It was bigger than the 9/11 attacks, especially, as some were speculating, if terrorists could take down the electrical grid.

Suddenly he heard Ron's horn. It sounded like it was coming from the entrance to the subdivision. Grant raced toward that direction. He came around the corner and was horrified. He was hit with so much adrenaline that he became numb and tingly.

At the entrance to the subdivision was a crowd of about a dozen young men. They were walking into the Cedars, whooping and hollering. Waving their arms and yelling. Some had sticks, or something. A few had rifles. Hunting rifles or shotguns. They were right under the street light.

Dumbasses, Grant thought. Silhouetting yourselves in the street light. Grant was thinking clearly and was terrified at the same time. Instinct and training took over.

There was Ron's car about 100 yards inside the subdivision. Grant couldn't see him, but could see that his driver's side door was open. Ron blasted the horn again and then came flying out the driver's side with his shotgun. The punks started yelling, which was immediately followed by the sound of gunfire.

They were shooting at Ron. Actual shots! Grant couldn't believe it.

Grant drove straight toward Ron's car. He was more afraid of getting in a car wreck than he was of the shooting from the men. He felt a surge of confidence as he remembered Ted telling him that most bad guys are shitty shots. Grant punched the gas pedal and raced toward the gunfire.

Ron used his car door for cover and started firing into the air above their heads. Damn! That shotgun was loud. Lights started coming in on the surrounding houses. Ron shot five or six rounds at them. Grant wasn't sure how many; he was concentrating on getting in between Ron and the crowd with his car. Ron would need to reload soon, and that took a while with a shotgun. Probably too long for Ron.

When Ron stopped shooting to reload, the pack of men started to run toward Ron. They were about seventy yards from his car, still silhouetted by the street lights.

Grant's foot was all the way down on the gas pedal. He was driving straight into the crowd. He didn't really have a plan. He just kept thinking he needed to get between the crowd and Ron.

Grant flew past Ron and slammed on the brakes. He was about to plow into the crowd of men. He skidded and stopped about ten yards in front of Ron's car. Grant prayed that Ron didn't shoot him as he zoomed in front Ron, who had reloaded and was blazing away with a shotgun. The hours of training with the Team made it so that Grant wasn't bothered by the shooting happening all around him.

Grant could see and hear the crowd as it approached his car. They were about twenty-five yards away. Grant opened his door, jumped out of the driver's side, got behind the door, smoothly drew his pistol, and got in the kneeling position, using the car door for cover. The closest people in the crowd were now about ten yards away. Grant could see their faces. They were running full speed at him. So many of them. To Grant, they were just like a bunch of steel targets when he was at the range with the Team. Just pick one and then another and keep going. No big deal.

Grant put his front sight on the closest bad guy. The glow-in-the-dark three-dot sights told him exactly where the shot would go and the street light lit up the target, who was right on him. Grant got a good grip and pressed the trigger. He felt the recoil but didn't really hear the shot. The guy was hit, but kept coming. Grant put a quick second one in him; right in his chest. The bad guy stopped cold right in front of him, but his forward momentum kept him flying toward Grant. The others in the crowd were further behind the first guy, but close and getting closer.

Grant flashed back to his training with the Team. Shooting at those human-shaped steel targets was paying off. The men were moving, but they were just targets to hit. Grant shot them one right after another. Efficiently. It didn't feel like shooting a person; it felt like shooting steel target. After he hit a few of the targets, they quit charging him and started to turn around.

He felt someone come up behind him, and swung around, prepared to shoot whoever was attacking him from behind. It was Ron.

Grant turned back around toward the crowd, and realized he had used the cover of his car door for quite a few shots so it was time to find new cover. He looked around for any close-in threats. He looked behind him and Ron. He remembered Ted telling him that bad guys have a tendency to be where you least expect them, so search and assess after you shoot. Constantly look for threats.

There weren't any. By this time, Ron was up against Grant's car door for cover. Ron didn't have his shotgun, but he had his pistol in his hand.

"Stay here!" Grant yelled. Then he yelled, "Moving!" like he had with the Team. Ron looked at him funny. Grant suddenly remembered that Ron didn't know those commands. Ron looked at Grant as if to say, "OK, move if you want."

Grant ran to the rear of the car, around the back from the driver's side to the passenger side, and—now he was scared—popped up and fired toward the crowd. He didn't have a target; he was just shooting to keep their heads down.

There was no one there. They seemed to be gone. Grant fired fast until his pistol magazine was empty. Without even thinking, he yelled "check" ejected the magazine, and slammed in a new one. He racked his pistol and started scanning the area for additional bad guys, but he didn't see any.

"Get in the car and let's go!" Grant yelled to Ron. Ron got in the driver's seat and threw the car into reverse once Grant was in the passenger seat.

Ron had moved Grant's AR out of the passenger seat so Grant wouldn't smash into it. They backed out of the area quickly; Ron tried not to hit his own car in the process.

Ron quickly backed the car into the intersection of two streets about 150 yards from the entrance and turned around so he was now driving forward. He was driving toward his house when Grant said, "We have to go back to make sure they don't come back." Ron abruptly turned the car around, and they flew back to Ron's car stopped in the middle of the street. They stopped and jumped out of Grant's car. Grant saw his AR in the back seat. He grabbed it and used the roof of his car as a rest to aim the rifle, which was pointed toward the entrance to the subdivision. Grant wondered why he hadn't used his rifle in the first place. Why had he engaged targets with this pistol instead of his rifle, which would have been better? Because this is my first gunfight, Grant thought to himself.

A car came flying down the street from their left, and Grant swung around. That red dot and circle of his rifle sight was perfectly clear. He aimed at the driver and clicked off the safety.

It was Len's car. Grant went back to pointing his AR at the entrance toward where the men had been. Grant was more afraid of Len hitting him with his car than getting shot.

He was fully alive right now. Every sense — hearing, sight, touch, even smell — was on overdrive. He felt like Superman. Not that he was enjoying this; he just felt invincible.

There were no bad guys around and Grant had Ron and Len covering him. He started to relax. Then he remembered a story Ted told him about guys getting shot when they relaxed after what seemed to be the end of a gunfight. God, Grant was thinking so clearly. He couldn't believe it.

Once Grant knew where Ron and Len were, and that they had cover, Grant started scanning 360 degrees with his AR. He didn't want some piece of shit to run up behind him or to his side. He was determined not to get jumped. That would be embarrassing. I could never face the Team if I got jumped instead of searching and assessing like I knew I should be doing, he thought.

Grant started moving to various cover points on his car and then Len's as he made his sweeps. He was in a zone. He was acting out the training, only this was for real.

Grant saw some things in the street ahead of him. He couldn't tell what they were. There were about five of them, and some of them were moving. He didn't know what they were, but they weren't trying to hurt him.

Ron and Len were talking to him, but Grant couldn't hear them. His ears were ringing, and his hands were starting to hurt from gripping the AR so tightly.

Grant had to block the entrance. They would be back, and quickly.

"Move the cars across the street so no one can come back at us!" Grant yelled. Ron and Len looked at each other.

"Damn it!" Grant yelled. "Go! Now! Block this entrance. Go!"

They jumped into their cars and moved them so one car blocked each side of the street. No car could get through. Grant used Len's hood as a rest for his AR and he kept scanning the entrance area with the red dot and circle. He could start to hear people talking to him.

"Hurt. They're hurt," Grant heard Len say. What? Who was hurt?

Len pointed to the slow moving things at the entrance.

Oh, God, Grant had shot people. Oh, God. He had hurt people. For the first time, Grant realized that he had shot people, instead of just hitting targets.

Now it made sense. The things in the street were dead and the things moving were — now that his hearing was coming back — screaming... those were people. Oh, God.

Grant just stared at the entrance. The screaming. He did that. He hurt them.

He went into his trunk and got his first aid kit. He thought it was odd that he was compelled to try to save the lives of people who, just a few seconds ago, were trying to kill him. But he was a sheepdog, and this is what sheepdogs do.

He grabbed his first aid kit, threw it to Ron, and said, "I'll go up to them and cover you while you go see if any need first aid." Grant didn't want to walk up to the people he'd shot. He didn't want to see their faces. Not that he felt guilty; they were trying to kill him and Ron. He just didn't want to look at their faces. He was terrified of their faces.

Grant went first, sweeping the entrance with his AR. Ron was behind him with the first aid kit. The first guy wasn't moving. It was obvious he was dead. Ted had a story about that too, where a guy thought a Taliban was dead only to find he wasn't. Grant kicked the body. Nothing. Grant kicked him a second time. Hard. Nothing. OK. That one wasn't a threat.

They did the same with two others. Same thing.

Two moving blobs were heading into the woods outside the entrance. In the street light, Grant could see a wide blood trail from where they went to the woods. It was the weirdest shade of crimson he had ever seen. It was horrifying. There was some screaming in the woods. It sounded like two different screams. Grant didn't want to go into the woods, but he wanted the screams to stop. He didn't know what to do.

"We can't help them," Ron said. He motioned for them to go back. Grant covered Ron while Ron went back. The farther away they were from the gun fight, the more and more silly it seemed to be keep sweeping for bad guys. It was pretty obvious they had left, or were dead.

Grant didn't know what to do. He didn't want anyone to see him with an AR, so he put it back in his car.

He had to leave. He just had to leave.

"I've got to get out of here," Grant said.

"What? You can't just leave," Len said.

"I have to go," was all Grant could say. He got in his car and drove the two blocks home. He got one block before he had to stop, open his door, and throw up. He wiped his mouth on his sleeve and went home.

Grant hit the garage door opener. How many times had he hit that garage door opener and come home to pretend with Lisa that things were alright when they weren't.

Well, that was over. He was a killer.

Killer.

That word kept running through his head.

How could he explain this to Lisa?

Chapter 49

The Easter Bunny

(May 5)

Grant was in a daze. Everything was cloudy and exaggerated. He had a raging headache. He got in the door and Lisa was there, looking concerned. She had heard the shots.

"We have to go right now!" Grant yelled to Lisa.

"What?" She looked at his pistol on his belt. "Where did you get that?"

"I had to shoot some guys," Grant said. "Some bad guys. Trying to attack Ron." He realized he was yelling even though she was just a few feet away.

"What?" she asked for a second time. It was starting to sink in. She heard gun shots, her husband was on a crime patrol, and now he was saying he shot some guys.

Grant wanted to change out of his clothes. He was sure they were soaked with blood. He looked at them and they didn't seem to have any on them. But he was convinced they were soaked with blood and were… dirty. Dirty. Dirty. He realized he was freaking out. He needed to calm down. Suddenly, a really terrifying thought crossed his mind.

The police. Grant had just killed three people and apparently wounded some more. Maybe Ron hit some of them, but Grant had shot most of them. His mind was replaying the shooting over and over. He could see each one of the targets — people — as he shot them.

Police? What police? Well, for a multiple shooting, they might send someone over. But then again, they were battling some huge protests at the capitol right then. There probably were not any police available in a fifty-mile radius. That thought comforted Grant.

Grant's mind started racing. Would he be arrested in a few days when the police could come by? Would that gang, or punks, or whoever they were, come back? Would his guns get seized? He was only protecting Ron and the neighborhood.

"We have to go now," Grant yelled. "We have to go out to the cabin. These guys might come back or the police could show up and they won't understand." It was like an emotional dam broke in him. All his fears, all his frustration at no one listening to him, all his begging to go out to safety at the cabin. It was all coming out at once. Right now.

"What?" Lisa asked, obviously terrified by her bizarrely acting husband. "No, you need to talk to the police," she said and picked up the phone like she was going to dial 911.

"What police?" Grant said, at a normal volume now, instead of yelling. "They're busy now. We have to go."

"We can't just leave," Lisa said. "Cole needs his things. I need my things. Manda has ballet rehearsals," Lisa said.

Ballet rehearsals? Ballet?

Was this really happening?

Lisa kept listing all the reasons why they couldn't leave. "Cole needs his routine...all our things are here...we can't go. This will be over soon when the police can come out here." She didn't seem to believe that last part, but was saying it anyway.

Grant snapped back. "No, Lisa! Damn it! The police won't be out here. Things will not be back to normal soon, if ever." He was yelling again and couldn't stop. "No, Lisa, everything is different. You need to adapt to the situation or we'll all be dead." He felt a lecture on normalcy bias coming on and thought he'd save that for another time. It was time for the Easter Bunny speech he had rehearsed in this head for months.

The Easter Bunny speech was for when the shit had hit the fan and it was time to go. Grant would tell her that he had enough supplies at the cabin for months. He would tell her that the Easter Bunny had put them out there. That way he wouldn't have to get into a debate about him having foreseen this. Saying the "Easter Bunny" took care of all this would remove the "I told you so" sting from it.

"Honey," Grant started to explain in his calmest voice possible, "I have at least nine months of food out there. The Easter Bunny left it out there. And we have neighbors out there who will work with us. I have guns and ammunition there. It's extremely safe out there."

What? Lisa thought as she heard this. Some kind of stockpile out at the cabin? Why would someone do that? The Easter Bunny? Maybe Grant was delusional after the shooting. She saw that often in the ER. Lisa was thoroughly confused.

She thought Grant misspoke about "nine months" of food. He

44

was excited and must have meant nine "days" of groceries, she thought. It never occurred to her that he actually had nine months of food out there. Where would he get it? How would he pay for it without her knowing? Where would he store it? Lisa could not believe that he really had all that food out there.

"What are you talking about?" she asked. She was living in the "normal" world, where husbands don't shoot people, where the neighborhood is safe, and where there would be no reason to have nine months of food at some cabin in the country.

Grant could tell that Lisa simply couldn't process what was happening. She was extremely intelligent, but simply didn't know the things he knew. He thought he'd try to live in her world for a few moments right then to see if that would work to convince her. He lowered his voice and spoke as calmly as possible.

"Let's say this is all over in a few days and everything goes back to normal," he said with a shrug. "Ron saw everything and he can talk to the police so I don't need to be around to do that. After a few days, when everything is fine, you can tell your friends that you went out to your cabin because it was quieter. Call it a vacation. Tell them that I was freaked out after what I had to do with the looters."

Lisa wasn't listening to that last part where Grant was talking at a lower voice. He had yelled at her and she didn't like that. All she was thinking about was that he was yelling at her, had just shot some people, and wanted to go to the cabin, which was weird. She just stared at him.

"We're not going out to some country cabin," she said as she crossed her arms. "This is our home. You need to go to police and tell them what happened. I mean, why do we need to leave here?"

The reasons were so obvious to Grant but he was aware that Lisa didn't know all the things he knew. She hadn't known about the armed evacuation of the gun store a few hours earlier. She hadn't studied the LA Riots and the looting after Katrina. She hadn't studied the Russian collapse in the 1990s or the Argentine collapse of the early 2000s. She didn't know about the bankruptcy of the state and federal governments and what happens when tens of millions of totally dependent people are cut off from welfare. She didn't know about how much the government hated people like Grant and what they would try to do to people like him. She hadn't had conversations with a Green Beret about how to fight a guerilla war against a totalitarian government. He had been right about everything so far, about how the Collapse would proceed. He had the outside thoughts telling him things that always came true. She hadn't heard, seen, or thought of any of this.

Because she had made it clear that she didn't want to hear, see, or think about any of this. The more troubling things got, her response was to gravitate even more toward the "normal." Toward insisting on the "normal" and trying to force the square peg of current events into the round hole of "normal." Grant couldn't talk to her about this. When he did, she put her hands up to her ears and yelled at him.

He was suddenly terrified. He realized the gap between what he knew about the reality of the situation and what she knew was huge. In a split second, it all came together. They had been living entirely separate lives when it came to what was happening. He realized he needed to tell her what was going on. The stakes were too high now to try to avoid upsetting her. Too late for that; shooting people had pretty much taken care of that.

He owed Lisa an answer to her question of why they needed to go. He calmed himself, to the extent that was possible, and started explaining in his nicest, softest voice.

"You ask a fair question, dear," Grant said, amazed at how much he'd calmed down. "Why go? Because society is starting to break down, honey. Look at the evidence around you right now. We've never even had a crime in our neighborhood in the fifteen years we've lived here. No one has ever even called the police here. Now, tonight, we have a gang of God knows how many young thugs with guns charging Ron and me. They were trying to kill us. Don't you see what's happening? There are no police because they are fighting hundreds, probably thousands, of protestors down at the capitol."

She smirked like he was exaggerating the number of protestors. Grant said, "Yes, dear, I saw cars and people on foot streaming there this afternoon. These people are angry, yelling, screaming, and demanding their programs back. I talked to a guy a few hours ago who said that it was a running battle at the capitol."

"Who were you talking to?" she asked. He could tell she was trying to figure out if this was one of his weirdo conservative friends.

"A guy at the gun store when we were evacuating it," he said, deciding it was time to come clean.

"Evacuating?" she asked.

"Oh, in all the mayhem," Grant said, realizing how much he was going to get yelled at, "I forgot to tell you that my friends at Capitol City Guns called around dinner tonight and said they needed some armed guards while they emptied out their shelves. They're

46

hiding their guns. They know that armed gangs and looters will be coming to steal their stuff. Everyone wants a gun right now for protection."

"Armed guards?" Lisa yelled. "You? What were you doing?"

This wasn't going well. "It doesn't matter now," Grant said, hoping he could recover from this. "What matters is that people with things like guns are evacuating from the city and need armed guards to do it. With all the traffic jams, the semi trucks can't get through. The grocery stores only have about two days of food, and that's if people don't freak out and stock up, which they will. Hell, they already are. The power went off in the entire western U.S. for a few hours. That wasn't an accident. Whoever did that can do it again. And will. It might be the Red Brigade who just blew up Congress today."

"You're overreacting, Grant," she said. "What are the odds that there is a terrorist attack, power outages, and the grocery stores are out of food? That just doesn't happen."

Grant tried to keep his voice down. "You're right. That doesn't just happen. But it just did happen. Honey…Congress has been blown up. The Senate office building, to be exact. Go check the news." He handed her the TV remote control and continued, "You'll also see that right after the bombing, the power was off for a few hours all across the West and on the East Coast. Don't you see that this isn't just another day? It's a breakdown of things. Of everything. It might be temporary—God, I hope it is—but it's happening. It's happening, Lisa. We need to be ready for anything. Not just for our sake, but really for the kids." Grant paused. He wanted to gauge how she was taking this in. She was just quiet. He decided he needed to say one more thing. They, or maybe just he, needed to get going on the bug out to the cabin so this conversation needed to wrap up.

"Honey," Grant said, "for forty plus years of your life, nothing weird like this has ever happened to you. That's good. I have seen violence and horrible things. I understand that really bad things can happen. But you're used to things being normal. That's…well, normal. Normal is normal. That's fair."

Grant pointed outside, toward where the shooting had been, "But this is the one time in our lives where normal isn't there anymore. We need to take the situation as it is and deal with it. For the kids. For us. Let's go out to the cabin for a little while until this blows over."

Lisa was silent.

"You're crazy and this is stupid," she finally said. "You are overreacting. You just shot some people and you're not thinking straight." She paused.

"And I don't like the implication that I've been wrong about things," she said. "You are yelling at me and telling me I'm wrong and I don't like it. I'm not going out to your stupid cabin just because there's some protest." She folded her arms. "I am staying here, and so are the kids. You can go if you want. Don't ever come back."

That stung.

You know what you have to do. This is when you need to leave.

This couldn't be happening. Grant needed to convince her. "No, honey," he pleaded. "You need to come with me to a place that's safe with food. You need to come with me. We need to go tonight."

She started to cry. "I'm not leaving!" She fully expected him to give in. He always did when she cried. Always.

"Not this time, honey," Grant said in an amazingly calm voice. "Crying won't do it."

Lisa was stunned that Grant just said that. She started bawling. She was shaking and crying harder than he'd ever seen her.

All during their marriage, arguments ended when Grant hugged Lisa. She always interpreted the hug to mean she won; he interpreted the hug to mean he was doing the right thing by getting the argument behind them. Usually Grant didn't really feel like hugging her after an argument. But he did it because he loved her.

Grant could feel that this was the "hug moment" and he almost started to hug her, out of habit. But he stopped. He couldn't hug her. Not this time. Things were different. The country was falling apart, there was a riot occurring three miles away from them, and he had just killed several people attacking their neighborhood.

Hugging her would mean he agreed to stay put. And that meant dying. He had tried so many times to talk sense into her. If she couldn't see why going to the cabin was the only thing to do, then she never would; hug or not. The outside thought was right. He had to go.

"Too bad, dear," Grant said with a sigh. "I'm leaving. I won't take the kids, even though Manda wants to come. I won't use the kids as leverage to get you to come. If anything happens to them..." As mad as he was at her, he couldn't make her feel guilty for what he knew was going to happen in a few days in the city, so he stopped short of saying what he meant.

Lisa wanted to yell out, "Hug me, stupid! If you hug me, I'll go out to your stupid cabin for a few days." She needed the hug because that meant things were like they used to be. Things would be normal if he hugged her, and she desperately needed some normal. She needed that hug so badly. She waited for it. She didn't think she needed to ask for it; he should just do it.

"Bye," Grant said. "Please come and join me. Please."

She just cried.

Grant remembered what his Grandpa said back in Oklahoma. "Don't ever want something so much you'll do anything for it. You'll pay too high a price, in money or something else. Maybe your soul." That was exactly right. Grant wanted Lisa too much. He wanted to be with her and the kids so much. Too much. He could feel himself actually thinking about staying in the house — even with the riots, looters, and maybe the police after him — because he wanted them to be together. How stupid was that? Talk about paying too high a price for something. No.

Grant wanted Lisa to come with him, but he wasn't willing to pay a price like death or jail to be with her. People could say he "abandoned" his family if they wanted to. Lisa was making a choice. She was choosing to stay in a place where they would die or Grant would go to jail. Grant couldn't live with that choice.

He had tried several times over the years to change her mind. He did amazing things to make it possible for her to have a safe place like getting the cabin and stocking it with supplies. What else could he do? Seriously. What else could he have done for her?

Grant wasn't going to put a gun to her head and tell her to get in the car. People make stupid choices every day. She was making one today. He wasn't going to die for her. He would die to try to save her but not for ballet rehearsals.

It was weird. After Grant finally decided in his head that he would have to go to the cabin without her, everything became clear. He was relieved. He could actually think just about fighting off criminals, getting past any checkpoints that might be out there, securing enough food, roadblocks, and other "little" things like that. They were little compared to the mental weight of trying to constantly convince Lisa to come with him. He actually smiled. OK. This is how it's going to be. Play the hand you've been dealt and survive. Don't live by the "normal" rules because there is no more "normal."

Grant had a plan for this. Of course. He went out to his car, walking past Lisa, who was crying, and got his list of things to take with him. He started gathering them up, including stealing Manda's cell phone. He had a use for that. He hoped that she didn't mind that he had stolen it. Given what was happening, it seemed like a small thing.

Grant's plan for the possibility that Lisa would not come to the cabin was to leave her some food and the .38 revolver with the red laser dot. He went to the garage and got the food out of his trunk that he purchased at Cash n' Carry earlier that day. Twenty-five pounds of pancake mix, a few big jars of peanut butter, twenty pounds of pasta, a case of big cans of pasta sauce, several hundred individual oatmeal packets. He put the food in a pile in the garage and put the .38 carrying case on top. He put an ammo can of .38 ammo at the base of the pile. He looked at the pile and said to himself, "So, twenty-five plus years together and it comes down to this."

The pile was a symbol of how Grant had failed. He couldn't convince a woman who supposedly loved him to leave a dangerous situation and come to a safe place. He had failed.

Deal with it, Grant thought. Deal with it because there will be more heartbreak and disappointment coming in the next few…however long this lasts.

Grant found Lisa in their bedroom crying. He said, "Come to the garage. There is something you need to see." She didn't want to come. She probably thought it was a dead body. That actually made him laugh to himself. Dark humor in a dark time.

"Fine," he said. "There's enough food for a month or so, even stuff you like to eat. It's in the garage." He added, sarcastically, "I'm so crazy that I got you all this stuff. Boy, you have a shitty husband, don't you?" He couldn't help it. It was so absurd. He was pissed at her. "I'm leaving you a gun. Manda will show you how to use it. You'll need it. Of course, you and the kids could be with me far from the rioting and with neighbors who will look out after us. But, no." He felt guilty for saying something that mean. But he was done trying to persuade her. He'd held back for years. He had nothing to lose. She was forcing him to leave. Making her mad was the least of his concerns.

Lisa just sat there crying. She couldn't believe this was happening. After a few seconds, Grant realized he was being mean to her. He didn't mean to do that. He had just slipped. Years of frustration were coming out. He regretting being sarcastic like that.

The fact that he had all that food and a gun picked out just for her made her mad. What an asshole, she thought. He was just trying to win an argument. Trying to make her look bad.

Grant was getting impatient. "I gotta go," he said. "I will load up my car with the last of my stuff and head out." That was it. The goodbye to their whole lives. Twenty five years of being inseparable. Having kids. Struggling through having an autistic child, law school, medical school, all the normal marriage bumps in the road. Dreaming about living the American Dream together and hopefully retiring some day in wealth and comfort. And it came down to this. Grant just walking out of the bedroom, leaving her crying. Leaving her and packing his stuff into the car. And, he didn't regret it.

He was just calmly doing what needed to be done. It was simultaneously the end of the world and a relief. He told himself, you tried. You tried hard. People make choices. She is making a choice. Dying is too high a price to pay for a pretty girl. Then he thought about what would probably happen to her in the city as it slipped into even more lawlessness. He knew what it would be. But he couldn't think about it. It was like she wasn't his wife anymore; she was just a woman crying in his bedroom.

Grant couldn't face the kids. They knew something was up. The sound of a mom crying will do that. He needed to talk to Manda. She needed to understand that he wasn't abandoning them. Good luck with that, he thought.

Grant popped his head into Manda's bedroom. "Manda, I need to go." He was talking loud enough for Lisa to hear. She needed to hear this.

"I have asked your mom to come to the cabin," he said in the artificially calm voice he had been using. "You know all the stuff we have there. She won't do it. She can't believe all this is happening. She's not a bad person, just someone who can't process all the horrible things that are happening. You guys can always come out and join me. We have plenty of food out there. Take care of your mom and your little brother."

Manda was quietly crying. She looked up at her dad and said "Can I come with you?"

What? Grant wanted Manda and Cole to come so badly, but wouldn't that be "kidnapping"? Grant felt awful enough "abandoning" his wife, but kidnapping their kids? That was too much.

"Honey, Mom needs you," he said as he went over to Manda's bed and hugged her. "Your brother especially needs you. I would love for you to come with me, but you need to be with them." He was so tempted to take Manda. And Cole. So tempted. But he couldn't bring himself to kidnap them. They'd be better off if he did; he just couldn't do it.

"Grandma and grandpa will be here and they'll help you," Grant said. Lisa's parents lived in Olympia now. "I don't want to get the whole family in trouble with the government so I'm…"

Leaving? He couldn't say the word. "So I have to go." Grant wanted to tell Manda things would get better in a few days and that the Collapse would be over. But he knew she was too smart for that. Saying it would just blow his credibility with her.

By now, Manda was bawling. Grant hugged her, tight, like it was their last hug ever, and whispered in her ear, "Try to get your mom to come out to the cabin. Please try. It's not your fault if she doesn't come, but please try. Please." Grant let go of her and walked out of the room. He felt horrible leaving his daughter this way. "Love you, dear. You're the best daughter in the world." He thought that was a better set of last words. He had to go.

He also needed to say goodbye to Cole. Innocent little Cole who just wanted to be tucked in every night by his dad. That would never happen again. That was the hardest part of all of this. No more tucking Cole.

Cole was crying because, despite not being able to understand everything he was hearing, he knew that Mom and Dad were really mad at each other. He understood that Dad was going away. He wondered if he had done something wrong to make his Dad leave.

Grant came into Cole's room. "Hey, little buddy, I need to go for a while. But I will come back as soon as I can. Or, better yet," Grant knew Lisa was listening, "you, Sister, and Mom can come see me out at the cabin." Grant thought he'd take a risk here: "Would you like to come to the cabin, little buddy?"

"Why don't you stay here?" Cole asked in between sobs.

"I need to go," Grant said. That is all Grant could think to say. He couldn't say that the police might be after him or that gangs might be coming back or that society was collapsing. "I need to go" was all he could come up with.

"When are you coming back?" Cole asked, still crying.

"Soon," Grant said. "As soon as I can. Actually, I bet you and Mommy and Sister come to see me out at the cabin. Bring your video games and movies. You can play with them out there. It will be fun, just like it always is when you come out there. You can throw rocks in the water like we do. Come out and your Dad will be there, OK?"

Cole nodded. Grant hugged his little man. God, that felt good. He would miss his son. Forever.

Grant walked out of Cole's room, and knew he couldn't leave without saying something to Lisa. He owed her that.

He went into their room—now, Grant, thought "her" room— and said, "You can come out any time you want. Just call me and I'll come get you. No matter how dangerous it is. I want us to be together. I just can't be here. It's too dangerous. I will never say 'I told you so.' Never. Please come out and let us be a family again."

She just bawled louder.

He never thought this was how they would leave each other. He assumed it would be on one of their deathbeds when they were old and gray. Not this way.

Chapter 50

Bugging Out ... Alone

(May 5)

Grant had all of his stuff in the car. All the guns, ammo cans, and his personal things. He had a list, of course, of all the critical things he needed when he had to bug out.

"Bug out." Yep, that was what he was doing. He had always imagined a "bug out" would be with his family. He would be a hero leading them to a safer place. At least that's how he imagined it.

But no. Now he was leaving them behind in a dangerous place. He was leaving them. Leaving them. His plan was failing. But what could he do? The reality was that it was dangerous in the city and his wife didn't see it. That meant his kids needed to stay. He was temped once again to go and just take the kids. He decided to go get them. He got out of the car and checked that his pistol was on his belt. He was going to take them.

No. Don't. Trust me.

OK. "I'll trust you with my family," Grant said out loud to no one.

Grant hit that garage door button and heard the familiar sound of the door going up. He'd never hear that sound again.

He backed out of the garage, like he'd done a million times before, going to work, running errands, taking the kids somewhere fun. No more. That was all over. He started to cry. Why couldn't she see how much better things would be if she came with him? At the moment she heard the garage door go up, Lisa starting wailing. She fell to the floor and curled up into a ball, screaming.

He was actually leaving. He was really doing it. He was gone. Leaving them here all alone. Why didn't he just hug her? She would have gone with him to his stupid cabin if he had just hugged her. But now he was gone. Probably going off to get killed or arrested. Who knows what would happen to her and the kids. Why didn't that asshole just hug her? He would rather get killed than hug her?

It didn't occur to her that he didn't know that all he needed to do was hug her. She never told him. And it never occurred to her that maybe she should have hugged him first. She was far too emotionally wrecked to be thinking straight.

Oh, God, Lisa thought. Grant would be dead soon. He was probably part of some right-wing group and was off to fight the government. Her husband had left her for… politics. Of all the stupid things to be left for. Politics. Another woman or ambition would make sense; that's what it usually was. But politics? The Constitution was a reason to leave a perfectly good wife? Lisa felt wounded. Betrayed. Traded in for something stupid.

The house was silent, except for her wailing. Pretty soon the kids were crying, too. It sounded like hell. The "wailing and gnashing of teeth" is how the Bible described hell. That's what the Matson house sounded like. The former Matson house.

After he backed out of the driveway and got onto the street in front of their house, Grant snapped back into reality.

Oh, shit. He had to drive through a war zone to get to where he was going. He checked his gas tank. There was half a tank, which was easily enough to get to the cabin if there was no traffic. Given the protests, riots, and crime — looting, maybe even — he didn't expect smooth sailing.

Grant drove past all the neighbors at the entrance of the subdivision. They waved him down. He just kept going. He saw the bodies of the men he'd killed. Boys, actually. When he got close enough, he could see they were teenage boys. White kids. They looked like dirtbags. They had those damned baggy pants down to their ass cracks. God, he hated that. Those baggy pants alone justified killing them. He chuckled to himself at the absurdity of that thought. He needed that humor to get through this. That chuckle broke up the mood so he could deal with all the things he needed to do.

As he drove close enough to see them, Grant looked at their faces. He knew he shouldn't. They looked asleep. With blood everywhere. They were not nice boys. Thank God for that. At least he didn't kill people who looked innocent.

Everyone tried to talk to him. He just kept the window up and kept driving, carefully so he didn't hit anyone, including the dead bodies.

His neighbors were looking at him strangely. They were pointing and whispering. They were looking at him like…he was a killer. They were afraid of him. They had slight fear in their eyes. They were treating him like a killer. He wasn't welcome in normal society anymore. He could feel it.

His neighbors looked like people he had known decades ago. His life as Grant Matson—family man, attorney, and resident of the Cedars—was over. These people had known a different Grant Matson. The first Grant Matson. The second Grant Matson was driving that car. He had business to take care of. He drove past like he didn't know them. Because he didn't. Except Ron. He had saved Ron's life that night by risking his own. He nodded at Ron, who was trying to talk to him. Grant kept driving.

Once he left the Cedars, he didn't see another car until he hit the freeway. As he approached the street that led to the onramp near the old brewery, he could see there was a big a backup on the freeway. It passed right by the Capitol. There were lots of police cars trying to get there and ambulances leaving. Grant had an alternate route planned. He got off the street before it fed onto the on ramp. He took a back street to get to an onramp to the highway leading to the cabin. No traffic at this entrance. Grant smiled. At least one part of the plan was working. So far.

He got onto Highway 101 and accelerated to cruising speed. He was staying at sixty miles per hour because he had a loaded AR in the seat and didn't want to get pulled over. That was probably not a problem given that the police were all at the capitol, but why risk it.

Grant needed some music. He hit the play button and one of his favorite "survival" songs came on, Long Hard Times to Come by Gangstagrass. The lyrics seemed to be speaking directly to him as he left his family behind to go off to the cabin to... survive?

> On this lonely road, trying to make it home
> Doing it by my lonesome
> Pissed off, who wants some?
> I see them long hard times to come
>
> Ain't got no family, you see there's one of me
> Might lose your pulse standing two feet in front of me
> I'm pissed at the world, but I ain't looking for trouble
> Think about it, nobody wants to die
>
> I'm ready to go partner, hey I'm on the run
> The devil's hugging on my boots that's why I own a gun
> This journey's too long, I'm looking for some answers

So much time stressing, I forget the questions

You probably think I'm crazy, or got some loose screws
But that's alright though—I'm a' do me, you do you
So how you judging me? I'm just trying to survive
And if the time comes, I ain't trying to die

Hey this is the life of an outlaw
We ain't promised tomorrow—I'm living now, dog
I'm walking through life But, yo, my feet hurt
All my blessings are fed, man I'll rest when I'm dead
Look through my eyes and see the real world
Take a walk with me, have a talk with me
Where we end up—God only knows
Strap your boots on tight you might be alright

On this lonely road, trying to make it home
Doing it by my lonesome
Pissed off, who wants some?
I see them long hard times to come

That summed it. Grant saw "them long hard times to come."
He was doing it by his "lonesome."
        The drive out to the cabin passed like the blink of an eye and
felt like a lifetime at the same time. Along the way, he thought about
his entire life. He thought about Lisa and the kids all alone in the
house. God, he wanted to go back. But he couldn't.
        Maybe he could.
        No, he couldn't. He knew he couldn't.
        *You have a job to do out here. You would not be safe back there. You
will be here.*
        What was this outside thought, anyway? Was it just Grant
saying to himself what he wanted to hear? But it wasn't him doing the
talking. Actually, no one was talking. It wasn't a voice. They were
thoughts but not Grant's. Oh well. The outside thoughts had been right
so far. They had told Grant to do some things that seemed crazy at the
time but now seemed very wise. Like getting prepared.
        Grant thought about the sheeple back in town. They'd be
clawing each other for the last Doritos in a few days. Maybe they
already were.

58

Chapter 51

The Hideout

(May 5)

When Grant got to the cabin, he wanted to make sure it was ready for Lisa and the kids when they came.

What a stupid thought. They weren't coming. Grant felt foolish for even thinking that.

But he couldn't deny that he was in a hurry to get out there. To get away from what was going on in the city.

He couldn't get Lisa and the kids out of his thoughts. He had always thought he would be so glad to bug out to the cabin and arrive there after escaping from the chaos in the city. He would be arriving at an oasis of security in a violent world.

But that had always assumed his family would be with him. He had always envisioned that he could convince Lisa to come. He had tried to mentally prepare himself for bugging out without her and the kids but he must have done a poor job of it. Bugging out without them was a shock to him. He felt like his whole detailed plan for surviving a disaster was now thrown off. A key element—his family—was not going as planned. He had months of food, but no one to feed.

As he rounded the road that led down to the water, his tactical sensibilities took over. Were there cops there waiting for him? That was completely unrealistic, but he had to start being careful about things like that. He was in a fight right now. He had his fighting wits about him. Like when he was walking around the neighborhood after his dad chased him with the knife and he used that dog collar as a makeshift weapon.

This fighting mode seemed rather natural for him. It was like old times. As much as his childhood sucked, he was seeing that it had equipped him to do things that most other "normal" Americans couldn't do.

He stopped his car at a safe and very dark spot a few hundred feet from the road that turned onto his cabin's short private road. He was going to give this a look on foot. Should he bring his AR? Would that scare a neighbor that he didn't know and...what? Would they call the police? Like the cops could leave the protests at the capitol and come zooming out to the sticks of Pierce Point because someone saw what appears to be the shape of a man with an "Army gun"? Nope, Grant was in a fight right now and wouldn't show up to it without all the tools he had.

He got out of the car and quietly closed the driver's side door. He did a press check of his pistol and checked to verify that he had his two mag pouches with two magazines each. That should get him through the next few hundred yards of road. He quietly opened the passenger door and retrieved his AR and shoulder mag bag. That had four 30-round AR mags and four more pistol mags. He did a press check on his AR. Even in the low light he could see a shiny brass cartridge case in the chamber. He verified that the AR safety was on. He ejected the magazine and checked it. It was full.

He carried the AR with his right thumb on the safety lever at all times. He could flip that off in a millisecond, if necessary. That's how he practiced; he'd done it a thousand times.

He looked through his red-dot sight; it was still on. He hadn't turned it off since the shooting. Oh well, the battery life was nearly 600 hours and it turned off automatically after twelve hours. Grant realized he'd be keeping this on most of the time, at least at night.

Grant charted out a course from his car to the cabin. He would hug the side of the road away from the water. It had the most trees and was the darkest. The lights were off in all the cabins.

He looked down at his feet to the extent he could see them. He had his good old hillbilly slippers on. And his 5.11 pants. Thanks goodness he had come from the neighborhood patrol a few hours ago and was in his "gun clothes." He didn't want to walk in the dark without proper footwear. What if he were in a suit? He laughed at himself. He wouldn't be in a suit for a very long time, if ever again at all. He was living in a 5.11 and hillbilly slippers world now.

Grant started moving. He was surprised at how quietly he could walk. He was listening for any sounds. It was weird how heightened his sense of hearing was. He didn't want any dogs to bark.

He slowly made his way to the county road. He had forgotten how long it took to go a few hundred yards when trying to be quiet. There was not a sound or sign of life from any of the cabins so far. Good. The place was probably abandoned, except for the Colsons and Morrells. He wouldn't wake them up. They might shoot him by mistake. Let them sleep. He'd go over in the morning. He would need a story to tell them about why he was here without Lisa and the kids. He started to work on one while he moved slowly down the county road. He wasn't coming up with a good one.

Grant got to the end of the county road where the gravel road to his cabin began. He saw his cabin. It was dark and empty. He didn't need to move as cautiously now. He was almost there.

He walked up to the cabin and onto the deck to the front door. He let his AR hang on his chest sling, got his keys out, and slowly opened the door. He walked in. The kitchen light was on and it partially lit up the cabin. Grant thought he'd turned that light off when he left last time.

Who the hell was that?

There was a man with a pistol pointed at Grant's head. Grant could see the shape of the man and the gun, but not the man's face.

He knew he was captured at this point. He didn't want to be tortured. It was time to die. Grant clicked off the safety of his AR and started to shoulder it at the man.

"Nope, partner," the man said quickly and waved his pistol from side to side. "Not tonight."

Grant knew that voice. Could it be?

It was Chip. What the hell was he doing here and how did he get in?

Grant was frozen with this AR halfway up to his shoulder. He didn't want to shoot Chip, if that's really who was in his cabin.

"That you, Chip?" Grant whispered.

"Yep," Chip said, still holding a pistol to Grant's head. "How are you Mr. Matson? Why don't you lower that rifle so there's no friendly fire here tonight?"

That was definitely Chip's voice.

Grant lowered his AR and clicked the safety back on. He let the rifle go, but it was on a sling so it just dangled. Grant instinctively put his hands out to his sides.

"Where's the damned light in here?" Chip asked.

"Behind you is a lamp," Grant said.

After some fumbling, Chip turned it on.

There he was. Chip and his .45. In Grant's cabin.

"What the hell are you doing here?" Grant asked.

"Storing some valuables," Chip said, wondering why Grant didn't know the answer already. "Just like we talked about when I was out here this summer. You remember, don't you? I mean, it's cool for me to leave some hardware here, right?"

Grant thought about it. Of course. Chip was stashing the guns here. Great.

"Oh, yeah," Grant said. It took him a little while to recover from the shock of a man in is darkened cabin pointing a pistol at his head. "Sure, it's cool," he finally said. "I was just a little surprised by the whole guy-in-my-house-pointing-a-gun-at-me thing. How are you and what can I do to help?"

Chip smiled. "All the hard work is done. I pulled in after dark, after we hauled my load from the store. I came straight here. Sorry for telling you and the other guys that I was going somewhere no one knew of. This shit is worth some money and…well, anyway, your neighbors weren't around so I unloaded this stuff in the dark. I got in with the key under the rock on the bulkhead. You know, the one you showed me. I moved my truck and the empty U-Haul to a spot no one would see about a half mile away. I didn't need an empty U-Haul sitting at your place. Tends to lead to questions we don't need."

Chip sat down on one of the two couches in the living room of the cabin and continued. "Right after I walked back from my parking spot, I was getting ready to try to sleep and I heard you coming in. You didn't exactly sneak quietly up on me. I figured it was you because you probably were the only one with a key. I had the bulkhead rock key with me so I knew it wasn't someone else who knew about that key. But I didn't want to be wrong so I had to draw on you. Sorry about that, but I'm sure you understand."

"Yep," Grant said. "I woulda done the same."

"So what brings you out here without the family?"

Grant felt a sting go through him. He didn't want to answer that question. He was ashamed that he'd abandoned his family. "It's a long story and I'd rather not talk about it. Let's just say that this place will be my…" Grant pointed at Chip and said, "… our home for a while. I guess we're both hiding out."

"From what?" Chip asked. "The riots?"

"Well, I kinda shot a dude," Grant said with a laugh. A nervous, tension-breaking laugh. "Three, actually. Wounded some more. Looters. In my neighborhood. They were coming after me and my friend with rifles and clubs. About a dozen of them. I got the surviving ones to run away. I tried to get my family to come out, but my wife is living in a fantasy world of 'everything is normal and just fine.'"

Chip just thought for a while. "Sucks to not have your family, huh?"

Grant realized that he and Chip were in the same boat. No family. Grant didn't like that thought. But it was true.

"For a while," Grant said. "I will go get them or they'll come out. I hope." Grant just stared for a while.

It was silent in the cabin. Just then the soft sound of the refrigerator kicked on in the background.

"Well," Chip finally said, "now that there's two of us, we can have a guard duty schedule. Let me go show you the stuff in the basement and you can show me the locks you have and how to secure this place."

Chip put his shoes on and pointed out the door. He wanted to get this done and get some sleep. He was tired. He had been up all night. And, at almost sixty, his ability to pull all-nighters was waning.

"Let's go have a look," Grant said.

Chip was the first out the door and he carefully looked around before going outside. So did Grant. They tiptoed down the incline to the unfinished basement. Grant got his keys out and opened the door. He turned on the lights.

There in his basement were some of the tubs and gun boxes he had seen at the store. Neatly stacked. Cases of ammo stacked and sorted by caliber. Nice.

"Where's Ted and his load?" Grant asked.

Chip looked around and lowered his voice, which was weird because they were all alone in the basement. "Ted is, um, talking to some people." Chip was smiling. "That's all I can tell you. Let's just say there is some serious shit going down now. Very serious."

Oh. Grant had an idea what that might be but kept the thought to himself. No need to speculate and blabber. That was not very professional.

"Professional?" Grant thought to himself. What profession was Grant now in? A gun runner? Harboring a fugitive? Oh, wait, he was a fugitive himself from the shootings. He and Chip were officially outlaws now. Wow. From respected attorney to outlaw in a couple of hours. Things were changing, and they could never go back to normal. This was the second Grant; the new and different Grant. He was an entirely different person.

Grant and Chip talked about all the stuff in the basement. Chip had a clipboard and looked at his handwritten inventory sheet.

"Let's see," he said, putting on his reading glasses that he kept in the front pocket of his t-shirt. Chip always wore a t-shirt with a front

63

pocket. Tonight he was wearing his usual gray t-shirt with the logo of Capitol City Guns on the front pocket.

"I have twenty-nine ARs and two tubs of various parts," Chip said. "I probably have enough parts to make two or three more; I think I only have that many barrels. I have most of my AR tools here. I have about 250 AR mags. Some red-dot sights—some Aimpoints and EOs, and some cheap Chinese knockoffs—and some mounts for putting them on carry handles. Some attachable iron sights. A couple of AKs and a handful of mags and parts." Chip never liked the AK. Ever since Vietnam he didn't like those things. He respected their durability, but he just didn't like them.

He pointed at the stacks of ammo cases. "I have twelve cases of 5.56. Six cases of 9mm and three of .40. One case of 7.62 x 39 and some miscellaneous shit." Chip smiled, obviously proud of the haul. "That about does it." His smile got bigger when he said that.

"Wow," Grant said, looking at all those weapons. "Wow." That's all he could say. This stuff was worth a fortune, but it wasn't the money Grant was thinking about. Grant blurted out his first thought, "We can outfit a lot of guys with this shit. A lot of them."

Chip grinned and said, "Roger that. That's the plan."

"What plan?" Grant asked.

"You'll see," Chip said with another one of his smiles. He took off his reading glasses and put them back in his t-shirt pocket. He rocked back on his heels and said, "I'm sworn to secrecy for right now. Don't worry, it's all cool and legal. Well, not really legal but we're not going to go on a crime spree," he smiled and added with a grin, "unless you want to."

Grant thought he knew what the guns were for. It was on the path, the path of what he was doing and why he was put here. The path led to…it was too hard to believe, but he knew where it led. OK, society was melting down, he had this cabin, and now he had a basement full of guns. He also had a trusted friend with a plan, who had a friend who had even more friends and a bigger plan. It all made sense. To the extent something as insane as this could make sense.

But, things were different now. It really did make perfect sense. The old Grant would have never thought this was normal. But, now, those stacks of guns and cases of ammo were the new normal. And he was damned lucky to have them there.

"How do you want to secure this place?" Grant asked Chip. They talked for a few hours about the guard duty schedule, setting up noisemakers around the basement door, and other things to secure the cabin and the immediate area.

The sun was coming up. Whoa. Was it morning already? In early May way up north in Washington State, the sun rose at about 5:30 a.m.

"Care for some breakfast, my friend?" Grant asked Chip.

"Sounds delightful," Chip said. He was a thin guy and didn't eat often. But when he ate, he really ate.

From his frequent trips out to the cabin, which often included overnights, Grant had plenty of eggs and bacon. They fried up a big batch and talked about everything that had happened and how to hide out there. Grant was relieved to be talking to someone about how all the preparations they'd made were coming to fruition.

While they were serving up breakfast, Chip asked, "Do you have any orange juice?" Chip always had orange juice with breakfast. He had some during the day, too, and always brought some to have in the little employee refrigerator at the gun store.

"Nope, but I have a lot of beer," Grant said. "Let's kick off our outlaw lives with beer for breakfast."

Chip got a beer out of the refrigerator, held it up, and said, "Why the hell not?"

This was kind of fun. Then Grant remembered that Lisa and the kids were back in the city. He had abandoned them. No, not really, he tried to…he kept running this loop through his mind of accusing himself of abandoning them and then justifying why he hadn't.

Chip noticed the immediate mood change in Grant. "What's up?" Chip asked.

"Oh, nothing," Grant said. He didn't want to be a cry baby. Besides, Grant had a family (or at least used to). Chip didn't. Grant had it better than Chip so he shouldn't whine.

"Just dealing with some shit," Grant said. "Hey, let's eat and then figure out how we're going to do a bunch of stuff around here."

After talking for a while, Grant realized he'd been up all night. He was getting tired, but he was operating on adrenaline. He was crashing now that he didn't have that adrenaline running through his body after the day's events. All of a sudden, Grant hit a mental wall of exhaustion. He couldn't keep his eyes open.

Chip saw it and said, "Take a nap. I've got the first watch."

All Grant could manage to mumble was, "Thanks, man." He went into the master bedroom and fell asleep in his clothes, with his pistol belt on. He had never been this tired. He had never had a day like this.

Chapter 52

"He's gone."

(May 6)

When Grant left that night, Lisa heard the garage door go up and then back down. And then waited. She waited for it to go back up, meaning that Grant had turned around and come back. He would just leave for a minute and then return. He had done that a few times when they'd had really bad arguments.

But, the garage door stayed quiet. First, for a minute, then a few minutes, and then all night. It was the longest night of Lisa's life.

She cried so hard that her ribs hurt. She had the worst migraine of her life. Everything normal was no longer normal. She wanted the normal back. The normal of Grant being in bed with her, the kids not crying, the neighborhood being safe, the world being peaceful.

She looked at the clock. It was 3:20 a.m. She went downstairs to see if Grant was down there. Maybe he never left and was just sitting on the couch making her think that he left. She realized that was unlikely, but she was desperate.

Grant wasn't downstairs. She went into the garage to see if his car was there. His space was empty. It was real now. He actually left. In the space where his car belonged was a pile of food, a black square case, and green metal box. Those were the green Army boxes he put his gun stuff in. She looked at the sturdy shelf in the garage. It was empty. It used to have those green metal boxes—Grant called them "ammo cans"—stacked up and some big gun cases. They were gone. They looked like missing front teeth.

Why did he leave bulk food? She could go to the grocery store and get things, so why did he do that? The big box of pancake mix—twenty-five pounds—wasn't the same brand as the pancakes Cole liked. What was Grant thinking? Was he just running an errand for her by getting this stuff? But, he wasn't getting the stuff they ate. What was wrong with him? He got it during the day and didn't flip out after the shooting until the night. So he got this stuff when he was thinking clearly. Why didn't he just go to the grocery store? What was wrong with him? Why was he acting so weird?

Lisa went back into the house and turned on the TV. She needed some noise. The silence of the house was too quiet. It only reminded her of how empty the house had become.

The news was on. Grant must have left it on that channel. She hated the news. But, when she started to see everything on the screen, she couldn't change the channel. She felt herself enter a trancelike state.

Things were going crazy on the news. There were suicide bombings in Atlanta, Miami, Detroit, and Des Moines, Iowa. Des Moines? What did they ever do to anyone?

It appeared that China had caused the electrical grids in the West and on the East Coast to fail. The U.S. Government was denying it, but the news said that numerous sources "who wished to remain anonymous" were confirming it. They said that China could take down the power in any region of the country any time they wanted. Any time. Without warning. It was a computer thing. Lisa thought that the lines would need to be cut to lose electricity. There was a computer that controlled all this? That could be hacked? Who let that happen?

The news kept getting worse. The stock market had crashed. Again. Actually, the stock futures market in overnight trading had crashed, which meant that the stock market would crash when it opened that morning. If it opened at all. They said that the stock market probably wouldn't open in the morning. She started to think about their—well, now her—401(k). It was gone. All that work. Poof. Gone.

The next story on the news was about California. LA was overtaken by riots. There were fires everywhere. Soldiers and police battling with crowds. Lots of people with guns shooting it out with each other and with police and soldiers. People were running wild on Rodeo Drive, smashing store windows and taking everything. Hollywood stars were leaving LA in their private jets.

The government was trying to do something about all this. The Vice President came on live, in the middle of the night, and said that the President was invoking some emergency powers and would get things back to normal. The military was called into their bases. The reserves and National Guard were called up. The Vice President said that all police and emergency personnel were supposed to report to their stations. He said that Congressional leaders had called him and told him the President could do whatever it took to restore order. Then he said that America had been through hard times and always come out of it stronger. The Vice President seemed very confident when he spoke. That's because he actually believed it.

Lisa tried to absorb all this bad news. Everything seemed to be out of control. Then she got mad at Grant.

He knew this was coming and didn't do anything. He didn't insist that they come with him. He should have been more forceful. He should have just hugged her and they would be safe. One hug and they would be together. But he wouldn't hug her. She hated Grant. For the first time in her life, she hated him.

There was noise outside. People were talking and moving around. There was a loud knock at the door. She jumped. It was Ron. He wanted to talk to Grant about the shootings.

"He's gone," Lisa said. "Went to the cabin. Without us." She didn't want to admit it.

"What cabin? Whose cabin?" Ron asked. Lisa realized that Ron didn't know about the cabin; Grant had always been weird about not telling too many people about the cabin. She realized she shouldn't tell people about the cabin in case they wanted to go get Grant for the shooting.

"Oh, a friend's cabin," Lisa said. "Down in Lewis County. I don't know where exactly," she said, wishing that she didn't have to lie to her neighbors. But that asshole Grant was making her.

Ron said some more things, but Lisa couldn't really hear him. She couldn't concentrate on what he was saying; she was in a daze until he left.

Maybe she should take Manda and Cole to the cabin? No, that would be crazy.

She went up to the kids' rooms and hugged them. They were awake and very scared. Grant was awful. Why was he doing this to them?

She turned off the news and sat on the couch and cried until the sun started to come up.

Chapter 53

Uncle Chip

(May 6)

Grant woke up. He was in the cabin. Daylight was coming through the window shades in the bedroom. What was he doing there? Then he remembered that he had come there last night. He was in his clothes and had his pistol belt on. He couldn't believe he could sleep with a pistol belt on, but he had been so tired that he slept fine with it.

Grant got up and looked for Chip, who was outside. He was watching everything. Grant came up to him.

"Mornin', sunshine," Chip said. He pointed at Grant's pistol belt. "Sure you want your neighbors to see you have that?"

"Oh, they're cool," Grant said. "In fact, we should go meet them. They need to know why an ugly man is hanging out at my cabin." Grant motioned for Chip to follow him. As they walked, Grant asked Chip, "What do you want the story to be? They're cool and all, but you can't tell them about the inventory."

Grant stopped walking, turned, and looked at Chip. "Of course, man. No one—not a soul—will hear about the basement from me." Chip nodded. He knew Grant was serious.

They resumed walking toward the Colsons', which was about fifty yards away.

"I'm your uncle," Chip said. He was in his early sixties and Grant was in his forties. The uncle story would work.

"OK, Uncle Chip," Grant said. He noticed the pistol tucked under Chip's shirt. "You might want to lose the pistol when you make these first impressions with the neighbors." Chip nodded and went into the cabin and then came out without a pistol.

They walked up the stairs to the front door of the Colsons'. Paul, Mark's son, answered the door. He was so overweight that he was breathing hard just walking. It was daytime, so Tammy must have been at work. Mark came to the door.

Grant said, "Hey, Mark, I wanted to introduce you to my Uncle

Chip. He'll be out here for a while. Things are pretty hairy in Olympia. He and I came out to get the place ready for Lisa and the kids."

Mark looked at Grant's pistol belt. Mark had a revolver on a belt holster. Mark grinned and said, "Come on in, gentlemen. It looks like we have some things to talk about."

Mark had the news on. Grant and Chip just stared at the TV. The shit had, indeed, hit the fan. This was it. Wow. Things were coming apart at the seams.

Mark let them take in the headlines for a minute or two. "Yep, the shit has officially hit the fan as we used to say in the Marine Corps." They all quietly took in some more headlines. This was unreal.

Mark asked them, "How's Olympia?" Grant told him about the protests and that the cops were too busy to do anything. He didn't tell Mark about apparently killing three guys and wounding a couple others. Grant knew and trusted Mark, but why confess to what some might call murder? Besides, he didn't want Mark to think he was a killer. He didn't want Mark looking at him that way, like his neighbors did last night. He also didn't tell Mark about evacuating the guns. That would be stupid.

Mark pointed out the window toward the other cabins. "How are we gonna secure our places? I mean, there is basically no crime in Pierce Point, but things aren't normal right now. In normal times, the cops would take a half hour to get out here if someone called them. Now it will take a day, if they even come out, which I doubt they would. I think we need to carry at all times. What about a guard at the end of the road?" He pointed to where the county road turned into the gravel road. "You know," he said with a smile, "keep the riff-raff out. So, for guard duty that would be me, Paul, and you two. I bet John Morrell would do it, and hell, probably Mary Anne. That's six people. Four-hour shifts. Not bad."

Chip just listened. He knew the less he said, the less of a chance the "Uncle Chip" story would unravel.

Mark said, "Let's go talk to John and Mary Anne." They walked from the front door of Mark's house, which was up on the hill, down to the gravel road below where Grant's and the Morrells' cabins were.

As they came up to the Morrells, Grant looked up to the second story window and saw Mary Anne up there with a shotgun. He was reassured by that. She waved. They knocked on the door and John answered, also with a shotgun.

"Figured you'd be coming around," John said. "We have some

things to discuss." He looked at the stranger, Chip.

"Hi, John," Grant said. "This is my Uncle Chip. He's helping me get the cabin ready for when Lisa and the kids come out. He had to bug out of Olympia, too. It's pretty bad there." Grant retold the same stories about Olympia that he told Mark and Paul, except for the part about killing guys and evacuating the gun store. And about abandoning his family.

John thought the guard idea was great. So did Mary Anne. They planned a guard shift schedule. They would do the first few shifts in pairs so they could go over things like code phrases for family and friends who arrived and were OK to have out there. They had one Pierce Point full-time resident with Grant or Chip since the full-time residents knew things Grant and Chip didn't, like who the neighbors down the other roads were.

The Morrells, Colsons, Chip, and Grant spent the next few hours picking guard spots and fallback positions, alarms, hastily building a little guard shack for when it rained, coordinating which guns people would use, and generally going over all the details of the very important topic of guarding their homes.

The whole time Grant was thinking about Lisa and the kids. He was trying to use the work of preparing the guard system to take his mind off his family back in Olympia. It would work for a while and then his mind would drift back to his family.

He needed a plan to get his family out there, as unlikely as it seemed that it would be possible to pull off. He found that the best way to deal with a problem was to plan for it and work the plan hard. That's what he had done with preparing for the Collapse and, for the most part, that was working very well. There was just one piece missing: his family.

Grant came up with a plan while he was making the guard shack. It was risky, but just might work. He kept refining it in his mind until it was pretty solid.

By late afternoon, the guard system was set up. Grant and Chip went back to the cabin. They were very hungry. Grant fired up the grill and grilled some of the frozen hamburger patties they had. He had gotten a bunch of them a few days ago because it was early May and the summer BBQ season at the cabin was just beginning. He was glad he did; hamburger would be a rarity soon.

Damn. Those burgers tasted good. Three of them, apiece. They washed them down with a beer. Those would be a rarity soon, too.

Grant was tired and couldn't stop thinking about his plan to get the family out there. He was ready to get it going.

"Hey, Chip," Grant said, "I have some shit in my head to deal with. I'd love to hang out and have some beers with you but I need to be alone right now. No offense."

"None taken," Chip said. "I felt the same after a fire fight in Vietnam. You've been through a lot the past twenty-four hours. Take care of your head, my friend. It's what will get you through this. Remember that."

Grant nodded and headed into the master bedroom. He got into the bedroom, closed the door, and took off his 5.11s and his t-shirt. He stank. He had plenty of work clothes to change into because he had been bringing his old work clothes out to the cabin for some time. He got into an old pair of shorts and an old t-shirt that said "World's Best Dad." It had a handprint in paint from both Manda and Cole. They got him one of those each Father's Day when they were little. He didn't wear them often, but had brought them out to the cabin. Now they had a meaning. He was wearing that shirt to remind him of the good times.

Grant activated his plan. He found Manda's phone that he had taken. He had thought clearly enough to also take her phone charger and had been charging the phone all day while he worked on the guard project. Grant knew that in emergencies, when everyone is calling, voice calls take lots of bandwidth, and often go down. Texts take a fraction of the bandwidth, and can often still be used.

He had his phone with him too, but he had turned it onto "airplane mode" so it did not transmit and then he turned it off, altogether. While he didn't think the cops had the time to be tracing cell phones right now, why take the risk? He thought he'd use his phone for the contacts in it, but then he remembered he had made a hard copy of his important contacts, like the Team, and the copy was out there. That way he could keep his phone off permanently.

Grant grabbed Manda's phone and sent a text to Pow. It appeared to go through fine. His text described the plan.

Grant could finally relax a little. He had launched his plan. At least he had done something about getting Lisa and the kids out there. He went out to the living room and saw Chip getting his pistol belt on. "Time for my first guard shift. I'm with Mark tonight. See you in eight hours. Stay plenty armed. We've got invaluable treasure down in the basement."

"Roger that," Grant said. Then they went over the codes they would use to identify themselves and to give each other basic coded instructions. "Break!" meant someone was trying to break into the basement. Chip picked up one of his personal ARs, which was leaning against the wall by one on the downstairs couch. He had four extra magazines in the pockets of his Carhartt work pants. That AR leaning on the wall looked so weird, yet so natural at the same time.

A minute after Chip left, John and Paul came over. First they told Grant the news that mushroom clouds were seen in Israel and Iran. No one knew who started it, but it didn't really matter. They felt bad for all the innocent people who had just died. They couldn't help thinking about the other consequence: gasoline would be worth its weight in gold now. There had been more suicide bombings in New York and DC and elsewhere. Hezbollah, an Iranian-backed terrorist group that had been openly operating in Mexico with the drug cartels, took responsibility and said it was in retaliation for the strike on Iran. John and Paul said there were protests everywhere. People were furious that everything was coming apart. Grocery stores were being looted in parts of California, although the news showed video after video of calm at grocery stores. No news about Olympia.

Nothing seemed different out at Pierce Point, though. It was like the news was about a different country. At Pierce Point, it was just another beautiful spring day out on the water. The weather was perfect.

After the news update, John and Paul talked about what they came over to discuss, which was fishing in the inlet, and gathering clams and oysters from the beach. They had all the gear and knew all the spots. They would go out in pairs during the days and bring back some food. They all had some regular food stored up. Grant hadn't told them about his food stores yet; he was saving information like that for people on a need-to-know basis, but he knew he'd be telling his neighbors about it soon.

All the fish and seafood would stretch their regular food supplies quite a bit. Plus, fishing and gathering clams and oysters was relaxing in a stressful time. Mary Anne and Tammy, who was now back from work at the power company, volunteered to cook up all the goodies. They would have a group BBQ each night. Fresh salmon, clams, and oysters. After John and Paul left, Grant's phone started vibrating. It wasn't Manda's phone; it was his. He had turned the transmitter off so why was it vibrating? He looked at his phone. He had a calendar event on it. It said he had an argument in a court case tomorrow.

Work? Oh, crap. He hadn't even thought about his job for the past thirty-six hours. He laughed to himself. Work. Like anyone was going to work right now. There wouldn't be any judges at the courthouse to hear him argue his case about why the government broke some law.

Law. Courts. That was a lifetime ago. It seemed so artificial and abstract now. Having enough food for the next few weeks, not getting shot, being able to be with his family. That's what mattered now. It was the "new normal."

Between guard duty and fishing and seafood gathering, each person would be pretty busy. Good. Grant could stay in shape that way. He couldn't go to the gym anymore.

More importantly, they weren't sitting around waiting for the government to save them. Their little group was bonding and really pulling together.

You are in the right place with the right people.

The outside thought was so soothing and reassuring. Grant, in the middle of all this life-changing chaos, had confidence he was going down the right path. He relaxed when he realized that.

While he was thankful to be where he was and who he was with, he was also thinking about his preps. This was the big test. Did he think of everything? Could he improvise to solve the problems that would surely come up? Grant was actually excited to find out. He felt guilty that he was excited because he had just left his family to do all this. (No, he corrected himself, Lisa had left him by staying in an unsafe situation when a perfectly safe one was waiting for her.) But he couldn't deny that he felt excited by this new phase of his life. However long he might live. Two weeks? Who knows.

He planned on living through this, but things could get really nasty, very quickly. Two weeks, he thought. That's probably how long he'd live.

Grant realized that assuming he'd be dead soon actually made things easier. He wasn't afraid of things. He could just do what needed to be done. If someone were attacking the guard shack, he knew he could run up to it with guns blazing and save his neighbors. He didn't want to die; he just accepted the very real possibility that he would be gone pretty soon. But he wanted to see his family again. That was his goal for living at the moment.

Chapter 54

Don't Scare the Kids

(May 6)

Lisa was all cried out when the sun came up. She physically couldn't cry anymore. She was a wreck. She hadn't slept or eaten in at least twenty-four hours.

Lisa's life was over. Her life was about her kids and husband, and he had left. Bastard.

She didn't see this coming. It was like he had been hit by a bus. Suddenly he was gone and she was all alone to deal with everything.

She finally looked at a clock. It was 6:12 a.m. Her mom would be awake. Lisa desperately wanted to talk to her mom. They were very close, to the point that people said they were practically clones of one another.

Her parents were living in Olympia now that they were retired. They only lived a few miles away, but it didn't seem wise to drive over there. The phone would have to do for now.

"Mom, Grant left last night," Lisa said without crying. Only for a second, though. Admitting this to her mom made Lisa break down in tears again. After a minute of sobbing, she continued. "He killed some robbers. It was self defense. They were trying to attack him and a neighbor with guns and clubs. Then he came home and was acting crazy and said we needed to go to the cabin. He must have PTSD."

"PTSD?" her mom, Eileen, asked.

"Post-Traumatic Stress Disorder," Lisa said. "I see it in the ER all the time. After a stressful event, people do crazy things." Lisa had convinced herself that PTSD was the only explanation for why someone would think they needed to run out to a cabin. The more troubling part, however, was that this hadn't been sudden; Grant had been stockpiling food and guns, so he had been suffering from some mental disorder before the shooting. Lisa could not figure out what had been driving him to have food and guns out at the cabin. A mid-life crisis? Whatever it was, it was crazy. Full-on crazy. Grant was probably permanently insane. She had married a mentally ill man.

"He just left us here," Lisa said. More sobbing.

"I'm coming right over," Eileen said.

"Mom, I'm not sure that's such a good idea," Lisa said. "There has been a lot of crime."

"Not in our neighborhood," Eileen said. They lived in a really nice part of Olympia. "I'm coming over to help my girl."

They hung up and Eileen got in her car. The short ride to Lisa's house was smooth. No crime, no sign of any trouble. Things were strangely quiet, in fact. Very few cars were out on the streets.

Eileen was in for a surprise, though. When she came into Lisa's subdivision, there was a man there with a gun. What was that all about? Was he a plainclothes police officer? That was probably it. Eileen wasn't stupid; far from it. Like Lisa, she had an extremely high IQ. It's just that, like Lisa, Eileen had never experienced things like violence or the system not working. She was like so many other Americans during the Collapse: smart but completely ignorant when it came to how to stay alive when nothing is working.

Eileen drove slowly up to him and rolled down her window. The man with the gun politely, but firmly, asked her, "What's your business here?" He could tell that a nicely dressed lady in her sixties in a very nice car was no gang threat. She was probably visiting someone.

"I'm coming to see my daughter, Lisa Taylor," Eileen said.

The armed man said, "Oh, Grant's wife. You know Grant saved Ron Spencer's life last night? Go ahead and go in." He waved her through.

Grant had saved someone's life? That couldn't be the shooting thing Lisa was talking about. Maybe it was. Eileen then thought about the guard with the gun. How strange, she thought. He didn't have a badge, but he had a gun. That didn't make any sense. Then again, lots of things lately were not making sense.

She drove the last two blocks to Lisa's house. Her little girl was there in the doorway crying. It must be because Grant left. What had gotten into him? He seemed like he had a good head on his shoulders.

Eileen spent the rest of the day consoling Lisa. She also spent time with the kids, reassuring them that everything would be OK, and that surely, their dad would be home soon.

It was dinnertime, so Eileen decided she needed to go home and get some clothes to stay over with Lisa and the kids. They needed her. She said goodbye for now and left.

When she was leaving the neighborhood, a different man with

a gun was at the entrance. Maybe they were guards, Eileen thought when she saw a second man with a gun but without a badge. He motioned for her to slow down and roll down her window. He realized she was not exactly a gang threat.

"Will you be coming back?" the guard asked. He had a clipboard like he was keeping track of these things.

"Yes, in about a half hour," Eileen said. "To see my daughter, Lisa Taylor."

"OK, but be careful out there," the second guard said. "It will be dark in a few hours. You don't want to be out in the dark."

"OK, thank you," Eileen said. What was that about not being out after dark? Sure, there had been some protests or some political things going on, and some terrorist attack in far-off cities, but that hardly meant that terrorists were out roaming in Olympia at night. She thought the men with guns were overreacting. Maybe the men felt better having their guns. They weren't hurting anyone, so it seemed OK.

The ride back to her house was uneventful. Few cars were out. Eileen's husband, Drew, was waiting for her.

"What were you doing out there?" Drew asked her. "Things are dangerous."

Eileen was a little mad. "I was taking care of our daughter, who needs me," she said indignantly. What was with all these men being so worried about "danger" out there?

"I'm going back to spend the night with them," she added.

Drew knew he couldn't tell her not to take care of her daughter. Besides, Eileen would be driving before dark.

"I'll come with you," Drew said.

"Oh, that's not necessary," Eileen said. She thought he was overreacting.

"No, I will come with you," Drew said. He had already loaded his two guns, a duck hunting shotgun and a .357 revolver, and was ready for what might be coming. He had been watching the news all day and knew that things were getting worse each night.

"No!" Eileen yelled at Drew. She hadn't yelled at him in about twenty years. "Everyone needs to stop overreacting!" she yelled. "Lisa needs me and I'm going. Things are fine. This will all be over soon." Eileen stormed upstairs to get her things for spending the night at Lisa's. Drew knew he couldn't do anything about his wife driving out in possible mayhem. He went back to watching the news. No use even trying to convince her, he thought.

Eileen got her overnight things and left without saying a word to Drew, which was very unusual. On the way to Lisa's house, there was a car speeding up behind her. It zoomed past her and ran the red light. Crazy drivers.

Eileen came up to the same man who had let her out of the subdivision. He saw her and waved her through.

Eileen spent the evening and night listening to Lisa and doing all the grandmother things she loved to do, like making cookies and playing board games with the kids. She wanted to do all the normal things they loved; this would take their minds off of all the unusual things that were going on. She kept the TV off. There was no need to scare the kids.

Chapter 55

Mrs. Nguyen

(May 6)

Ever since the previous night, when they evacuated Capitol City Guns, the Team (minus Grant) was sticking together. They were on an adrenaline high. They were, after all, young men who loved to help people and had trained for this and were extremely well armed. Guns and training — and being sheepdogs — were the focus of their lives. This was "go time." It was what they lived for.

If Grant were twenty years younger and single, he would have had the same reaction, but he had a family so he didn't have the luxury of treating the Collapse as a big adventure. He couldn't think of himself; he had a family to protect. This adventurous spirit of young men is what had fueled wars and heroism for several thousand years. It was hardwired into some percentage of the male population (and some percentage of the female population).

After the Capitol City evacuation, Pow, Wes, Scotty, and Bobby met up at Pow's little rented house. It was located a mile or two from Capitol City and was a central location for the other guys. They lived in apartments throughout the city.

"How are your parents doing?" Scotty asked the group. "Mine called and they're OK out in the sticks."

Bobby nodded, "Mine, too."

Pow said, "My parents and all my brothers and sisters are doing fine up in Tacoma." Pow was the youngest of six kids.

Wes was silent.

With that out of the way, it was time to get down to business.

"Well, gentlemen, this is it," Pow said. "We need to protect our neighborhoods and our stuff." He pointed toward the "gun room" in his house. He had a giant safe and reloading equipment, with cases of ammunition on the floor. The contents of his gun room were now worth tens of thousands of dollars.

"We need to secure our gear," Pow said. "Things are going to get dicey, at least for a while." Pow thought things would be crazy for longer than that, but didn't want to seem overly dramatic. He was the leader. He needed to be calm and rational.

Wes said, "Yeah, but where do we take our stuff? We need to be with it. Hell, we might need all of our gear." Scotty was nodding.

"I have good news, my friends," Pow said with a smile. He told them about Grant's cabin. They were all grinning from ear to ear.

"I knew there was a reason we let a lawyer on the Team," Bobby said.

"So, let's come up with a plan to get our shit over to Grant's cabin," Pow said. "I have a call into him but his phone isn't working." They spent the next two hours carefully planning out how to load and move their personal armories. They prioritized the things they would need the most. The first priority would be ARs, 5.56 ammo, and pistols in 9mm, along with 9mm ammo. Mags, spare parts, and specialized tools for these guns would also be in the first priority. The other stuff — AKs, shotguns, bolt rifles, other pistols — would be in later loads.

"What about food? I don't really have any in my apartment," Bobby said. He was a basic bachelor in his twenties; not a "prepper."

"Grant has us covered out there," Pow said with a smile. "Everyone bring what you can. Food will be the last priority load."

It was late afternoon. "Go back to your places and load up your stuff and bring it here," Pow said. "We'll meet back here in a few hours. We can make the first run out there tonight."

Pow's cell phone vibrated. He looked at the number. He didn't recognize it. He'd look at the text later.

There was a knock at the door. They instinctively drew their pistols. Pow looked out the window and saw Mrs. Nguyen, an elderly Vietnamese neighbor lady. He holstered his pistol and the others did too. He answered the door.

"Hello, Mrs. Nguyen," Pow said.

"William, I am so scared," she said to Pow, whose real name was Bill Kung. She was one of the few people who called him by his real name. "I have been watching the television all day," she said, speaking English well, but with a Vietnamese accent. "This reminds me of Saigon before the fall." She had lived through the fall of Vietnam and came to America when her country fell.

"William," she said, "there won't be food in the store soon. People will buy it all, and then they'll fight over it. Same with gasoline. I've lived through this before."

She paused and started to cry, "My sons are in Los Angeles."

She knew what was happening there now and couldn't bear it. They hadn't called in days. "I need some help." Her Vietnamese pride made it hard to ask for help, especially from non-Vietnamese people. But there were none in the neighborhood, so a nice Korean boy and his friends would have to do. "I need some food and water to make it through this for a while. And some of my medicine. Can you help me?"

Who could say no to that?

"Of course," Pow said. "Me and my friends can definitely help." Pow introduced the group to her. "Give me a list of what you need at the store, and each one of us will go out and get those things. That way, we can each hit a different store and get what they still have available. I can take you to the drugstore since you need to show ID to pick up a prescription. You'll be safe with me."

Mrs. Nguyen looked at the nice young men there offering to help her. She cried some more.

Wes would hit the grocery store nearby, Scotty the one a little farther away, and Bobby the next one over from that one. Pow would take Mrs. Nguyen to the drugstore in his Hummer.

She had an envelope of $100 bills. She had been saving them for something like this. She gave two to each of them. Who knew what food would cost right now? Plus, she wanted the boys to keep the change.

Pow didn't even need to say it. They all knew that they would go with concealed pistols. The ARs would stay hidden in the trucks.

"Be sure and top off your tanks when you're out there," Scotty said. They all nodded.

"Let's go," Pow said. It was their first mission. Getting groceries and prescriptions for a nice neighbor lady. It felt great. They were sheepdogs. They were in a position to help. That felt even better.

Pow's neighborhood seemed pretty safe. He lived in a starter house in an OK neighborhood full of nice people for the most part. But on occasion, some questionable guests and relatives of the residents came by. Mrs. Nguyen got in Pow's Hummer. "So fancy," she said as she got in.

They all left in their trucks and Pow's Hummer. This was their first foray out into a collapsing American society. They had no idea what to expect.

They found things to be surprisingly normal. No looters, no gun fights. People were remarkably normal. Some of them seemed a little edgy, in a hurry, and not trusting of the people around them. It was like it never occurred to these people that things were going bad.

The Team was convinced that most of America was either stupid or in denial. Or both.

The stores were getting empty. Not stripped clean like they had all assumed when they thought about panic buying. Then again, it was only one day into the electrical grid attack and the terrorism. Most people hadn't figured it out yet. They assumed the stores had lots of food. Stores never ran out of things. That's just how it was in America.

Most shelves still had food, but only about a third as much as normal. Meat and produce was still available. The stores had everything on Mrs. Nguyen's list, except some particular brands of Asian foods. For the most part, her list had staples like rice and canned food. They bought as much as they could with the money they had.

Each man topped off his tank on the way home. The price had doubled in twenty-four hours. There was a long line. It wasn't a line down the street, just a line longer than they had ever seen. Wes had lived in Alabama during a hurricane and had seen gas lines like this back then.

Unlike the relative calm at the grocery store, people at the gas station were nervous and keeping to themselves. Scotty thought about how he wished he had gas cans to fill up. Then he realized other people might not appreciate that.

Pow's trip to the drug store with Mrs. Nguyen was a little more eventful. It appeared that many people had the same idea about stocking up on prescriptions. The place was packed. Luckily, the computer had Mrs. Nguyen's refill on file. They waited in line. Pow used the opportunity to get plenty of first aid supplies and over the counter medicines. Mrs. Nguyen saw what he was doing and gave him a $100 bill for them. Since he was Asian too, he knew that she would not let him pay for them himself. He tried the traditional three times to let her keep the money and then accepted it on the fourth try.

Some of the people in line were freaking out. One of them wanted pain medication, and was getting belligerent. It was uncomfortable for everyone there. Finally, the manager came. The belligerent man, who looked like a thirty-something professional, started to yell and wave his arms around. "My doctor said he sent in the refill. I'm going on a trip and need these right now. My back hurts." Pow figured he'd let the guy do one more outburst and then that would be it. The guy didn't seem to be armed.

Sure enough, there was one more outburst. When the manager told the man to leave, he shoved the manager. Pow set his basket of first aid supplies down and flipped up his shirt to show his gun and gripped his Glock in the holster. He did not draw his pistol; he just showed it and had his hand on it, ready to draw.

"Time to go, sir," Pow said in a very commanding voice.

Pow knew that in normal times, showing a weapon like that without being threatened would be the crime of brandishing. Pow was not terribly worried about the police coming right now. He needed this guy to get out of the way so Mrs. Nguyen could get her medicine.

The man went silent and instinctively put his hands up. The man knew he was done at this location. He would go try to the other store in this chain across town that had the same computer system.

Everyone in the store was silent, appearing stunned by what they were witnessing. The man kept his hands up and walked out. Pow followed him, with his hand still on his holstered pistol. A few steps into it, Pow used his other hand to pull out a badge on a dog tag chain around his neck so it was visible.

When the man walked out the door, Pow threw his shirt back over his holstered pistol and stood at the entrance. He said to the checker, "I'll make sure he doesn't come back." She just nodded. And stared.

Pow watched the man speed out of the parking lot. By this time, Mrs. Nguyen's turn in the line came up and the pharmacist provided her medicine.

"Can I get more than one refill?" she asked. From the look on his face, it appeared that the pharmacist had been hearing this question all day.

"No, ma'am," he said. "We will need another prescription for a new amount from your doctor. We can try to call him or her, but no doctors' offices have been answering their phones for the past couple of days."

Mrs. Nguyen nodded. She knew that would be the answer. "Thank you," she said. She picked up Pow's basket and paid for it and the prescription with cash, careful not to let people see her $100 bills. She left the store, meeting Pow at the exit. He had his badge under his shirt now.

"Thank you for making that man leave," Mrs. Nguyen said.

Pow realized that she hadn't seen his badge or she would have asked him why he had a badge but wasn't a police officer. A good question, but he had a good answer. Pow, and all the members of the Team, had badges that looked like police badges but said "Concealed Weapons Permit" and had their state seal. They carried these so that if they had to draw a weapon, they could leave the "badge" out on a neck chain for the police to see. The police would know that they were not criminals. It wasn't impersonating an officer because the badge only said "Concealed Weapons Permit."

"No problem," Pow said. They drove to the closest gas station. That Hummer got thirsty, but Pow loved it. It was an H2, so its gas mileage was like a regular SUV. He was very successful selling insurance to Korean families and didn't have a wife or kids. He could afford it and, along with his guns, his Hummer was his luxury item. Besides, the Hummer was almost bulletproof. Almost.

Gassing up was uneventful, but Pow noticed that people were nervous and seemed ready to fight each other. He could feel it. He grew up in a tough part of Tacoma and had learned early on to pick up on things like people not making eye contact or people looking one another up and down. He didn't sense any threats there, but he was watching.

On the way back to Pow's house, there was nothing noteworthy, except one car on the other side of the street was speeding and driving erratically. Some people were on edge and in a hurry, driving like madmen. Pow expected to hear a siren. The police would be chasing that person. Then he thought about it. He hadn't heard any sirens lately. Last night when they evacuated Capitol City Guns, he had heard them in the distance. But now he wasn't hearing them. They had just stopped. Weird.

One by one, the rest of the Team returned to Pow's house and unloaded the groceries at Mrs. Nguyen's house. They tried to hide the bags as best they could so the neighbors wouldn't see. She wouldn't take the change back. As they were unloading, they smelled something delicious. She was making a big dinner for the hungry young men who had helped her.

"Won't you stay for dinner?" she asked.

They all looked at Pow for a signal on whether they should stay. "Of course, Mrs. Nguyen," he said. Helping people wasn't always about protecting them with guns; sometimes, it was sharing a meal with a nice lady.

Over dinner, Pow told the story about the druggie. "Then I pulled out my concealed carry badge," he said and he demonstrated it to them.

Mrs. Nguyen came into the dining room and saw Pow's badge. She was very surprised. "Oh, I didn't know you were police."

"I'm not," Pow said. He explained why they carried the badges.

"Very smart, William," Mrs. Nguyen said.

They ate the best meal they'd had in quite some time. They hurried a bit because it was getting dark and they were concerned that they were losing valuable time sitting there instead of bugging out.

Pow looked at his watch. "Well, it's time for us to go. We have some things we need to do soon."

"I understand," she said. "Thank you again." With that, they left.

Chapter 56

Secure Location

(May 6)

The day before, when the protests started, Jeanie Thompson had been trapped at her State Auditor's office, which was adjacent to the rotunda of the capitol building. The protestors encircled the rotunda. It was the most exciting and frightening time of her life up until that point.

She and her colleagues were constantly watching the news and passing along rumors. The Governor's Office was receiving dozens of telephone threats. They evacuated the Governor's Mansion and gubernatorial senior staff offices. The House and Senate buildings were evacuated. Staff at the capitol were told to work from home.

There were many strange security measures taking place. Jeanie noticed that as soon as a car left a parking spot, a traffic cone would appear in the spot so no one could park there. Was that to keep car bombs away? She also noticed swarms of state police patrolling around, some with dog teams. They did not have rifles with them; they were trying not to alarm anyone. There were loud protests outside, but only with a few hundred people, which was not entirely unusual for the capitol. The size of the protests seemed to grow every hour until Jeanie started seeing crowds bigger than she'd ever seen.

There was a helicopter whirring overhead most of the time. Unmarked state patrol cars were zooming around with people in the back; probably legislators and other elected officials. None of this was going on the day before. Today was different; definitely different. The State Auditor's Office had a state patrol trooper assigned to it. This duty was usually assigned to a new trooper because it was easy, largely consisting of walking around the office and waiting area and being alert. But now it was a bigger deal. There were many people furious at government. Most of the angry people were losing benefits and were desperate, but some were mad because government was taxing them too much. The state patrol knew that most attacks on politicians and their staffs were from angry and desperate individuals. Jeanie knew their trooper, Mike Vasquez. He had been there for a few weeks. He was about Jeanie's age, in his mid-twenties; kinda cute, she thought.

Mike, or "Trooper Vasquez" as she called him when people were around, was very focused today. "Good morning, ma'am," he said to her in his official trooper voice.

"Good morning," she said. "So what's going on today? Things seem rather tense." She was very curious, but was also looking for information to put into the rumor mill. He was cute, as well, so talking to him wasn't exactly a chore.

Trooper Vasquez knew plenty that was going on, but specific information on threats was distributed through official channels. However, there were general things that he was authorized to tell the protected employees for their own safety.

"We have received numerous threats to the Governor, Legislature, and other elected officials, including the State Auditor," he said. That last part about Auditor Menlow being threatened was news to Jeanie. What Trooper Vasquez didn't say was that there were only about two dozen threats, most from obvious lunatics who weren't a real threat, but a handful of threats were shutting down the government. That's all it took. For years, government had been convincing itself that the citizens were a threat to it. Government had developed a bunker mentality that everyone was out to get it. That was silly paranoia. Until now.

Trooper Vasquez continued, "We are implementing our plan for this. You might have seen abnormal activity. We are preparing for some large protests this afternoon. We will close the capitol campus at noon. Everyone needs to go home. Please let your co-workers know. Please report any suspicious activities or people, and especially any packages left unattended, to me or another trooper. We have dog teams coming through to sniff for bombs."

Wow. This was serious, Jeanie thought. She thanked him and went into her 8:30 a.m. executive staff meeting with the State Auditor. The meeting was chaos.

A thirty-something cute guy with dark brown hair from the Governor's Office was there. Jeanie thought that was weird. They had never been briefed by the Governor's Office about anything.

The young man started the meeting by introducing himself as Jason and abruptly saying, "Sorry, but I have to go in a few minutes. The Governor wanted you to know what is going on. We're shutting down state government for…" he paused, "a while." He quickly added, "Essential services will continue. Law enforcement, prisons, that kind of thing. Other state employees will be sent home today or tomorrow. There's no use having them around. No one is getting any work done. Some are calling in sick now that they have family to worry about."

Jason seemed uncomfortable about this next part. "The Governor has been moved to a secure location." He turned to Menlow and said, "Sir, you are fifth in the line of succession." Jeanie knew that the state constitution had a line of succession for when there was a vacancy. She knew that it went something like Governor, Lieutenant Governor, Secretary of State, Attorney General, somebody else, and then the State Auditor. They had always joked about it with Menlow, saying "you're just five heartbeats away from the Governor's Mansion."

Jason continued, "Mr. Auditor, you need to be in a secure location. You can bring your immediate family and two staff members. That's it. You need to tell your trooper who is coming with you. Your guests will need to have all their personal effects and some photo ID and be here by noon."

The room fell silent.

Menlow just nodded slowly. He was taking it all in. He felt that adrenaline surge. He loved this. "Secure location" and body guards. He felt so much like the Governor already. This was fabulous. During the upcoming campaign season, he could say that he had been evacuated with the Governor. That would get him votes. People would view him as a key player in a crisis. This was awesome. He wanted to smile but didn't since it would have been wildly inappropriate.

"I'll take Tony," Menlow said. That was his Chief of Staff, Tony Walker. Jeanie didn't actually know Tony well, but knew that he was a long-time state agency manager. He wasn't a Kool Aid-drinking Democrat; he stayed out of politics and basically managed people. Jeanie thought he was a nice, but boring, guy. He was about to retire, so Jeanie didn't pay too much attention to him. She had a direct connection to Menlow—getting him elected and trying to get him elected to the next job—that put her outside of Tony's control.

"And Jeanie," Menlow said.

Jeanie felt a surge of pride. She had made the traveling squad. Of course he picked her. He needed political advice now even more than ever. She nodded to Jason.

She thought about her boyfriend, Jim. He was deployed now, anyway, so she didn't need to worry about that. Her cat could stay with a neighbor. She didn't have kids, so she was free to go have a big adventure. A scary adventure, but a once-in-a-lifetime one, nonetheless.

This would be so awesome when everything calmed down, she thought. "Let me tell you the story about when I was evacuated to the Governor's secret location during the protests," she would tell people. How cool was that?

Jason looked at his watch and said, "I need to go brief the Secretary of State in a few minutes." He had to give the mandatory pep talk part now. "This is just a temporary thing. A few days. The protests will peter out. People are mad, but soon they'll realize we all need to make some sacrifices. We're Americans. We'll get through this."

Jeanie was mentally rolling her eyes. That spiel might have worked on her a few years ago when she was a flag-waving Republican. But, the more she saw firsthand how government really worked, the more she knew why the country was in the situation it was in. And she knew the country wasn't just going to "get through it." America wouldn't get through this in one piece with things being like they had been. America would be a worse place when all was said and done.

Jeanie hated to admit it, but the more she was in the upper levels of government, the more she wanted the "secure location" kind of perks. She loved being briefed by the Governor's Office. She felt so important. She really liked the idea of being *Governor* Menlow's press secretary. Really liked it.

Jeanie and the rest of the staff of State Auditor's Office were lucky they left the office early that day. That evening, the same evening the Team evacuated the gun store, a giant protest enveloped the capitol. Most state office buildings on the capitol campus were vandalized. Some had small fires. The few state employees remaining in their offices were dragged and beaten. One died. This was serious.

Chapter 57

The Mailroom Guy

(May 5)

The protestors didn't just plan to attack state offices. A few of them, the most rabid left-wing union organizers, planned to go after WAB's building, too. They had always hated WAB and now it was payback time. Besides, the cops couldn't stop them, so why not trash the place?

WAB's office building was beautiful. Nestled in the historic district of Olympia, it was a former brick mansion of a timber baron from days past. It was on the registry of historic buildings. The former mansion was a brick building with two huge trees in the front. Inside, the building had ornate woodwork. The office was majestic and grand.

A few hours before the protests hit, Tom Foster had sent the WAB employees home. He wanted to stay there because he felt like the captain who had a duty to go down with the ship, but that would be stupid. He knew these protestors would be vicious. Having grown up poor in Detroit, he understood violence.

As noon approached, the last people in the office were Tom, Brian, Ben, Eric, and Carly the young intern. So was Jeff Prosser, the mailroom guy.

Jeff was an interesting guy. Most mailroom guys are. Either they are in a band or are working on a book. Either way, they're interesting. Jeff was a part-time WAB employee and was a full-time farmer. He had a small farm out in the sticks, about ten minutes from Olympia. He was a country boy, and really smart.

Over the past few weeks, Tom noticed that Eric had been getting more agitated and angry. He really hated the government. Everyone understood why and agreed that things were bad, but Eric was taking it personally. Sometimes Tom wondered if Eric would go off and attack someone. That afternoon, he came into Tom's office where Brian, Ben, and Jeff were and began to say some disturbing things.

"This is it, guys," he said excitedly. "It's on," he said, referring to the next wave of protests that would coming in a few hours. He started to yell. "Now's our chance to smash these assholes in the mouth. Beat them down. They have destroyed this country." He looked at all of them for support. They just stood there. Smashing mouths? That seemed a little over the top. Eric was scaring everyone in the room.

Eric went on, "I'm going to mix it up with these protestor shit bags. Who's in?" No one said anything at first.

Tom said, "You should go home, Eric. I hate these people, too, but you'll be outnumbered…"

"I'm sick of being outnumbered!" Eric yelled. "I'm sick of it. The libs should be afraid of us. We outnumber them!" He stormed out of the office.

Ben said, "He's just a little amped up with all that's going on. Let's get on with this and go home."

Jeff closed the door to Tom's office. Carly was a few offices away down the hall. Jeff liked Carly but he didn't know her well enough for her to be hearing what they were there to talk about.

Jeff handed each of them a piece of paper. He and Tom had worked out a plan a few days earlier when it looked like things might be going bad.

"Here are the directions to the Prosser farm," Jeff said. He had a few extra copies and tore them up. "I'm not real interested in the protestors finding these and coming out," he said.

Brian asked, "You have enough space for three families?"

"Yep," Jeff said proudly. "We have a big old farmhouse, and a guest house. No problem. Just bring yourselves. Any extra food and guns you have would be welcomed."

"What about gas? I'd rather not have gas cans in my car with my kids in there," Ben said.

"Got you covered," Jeff said with a big smile. "I have 500 gallons of diesel in my farm tank. I use it for the tractor, but it also works in my diesel pickup and Jeep." He paused and grinned, "Of course, it's dyed off-road diesel so it would be illegal for me to use in a vehicle off the farm." He was referring to pink-dyed fuel for off-road use that was not subject to the highway fuel tax and therefore couldn't be used in vehicles that went onto the highway. Given what was going on right now, worrying about a law like that seemed so silly.

Brian said he wasn't sure his wife would like staying out at a farm. "Remember, this is only temporary. Maybe a day or two until the protests calm down. No offense, Jeff, it's just that my wife is a city girl and probably won't react too well to this farm thing."

"Understood," Jeff said. "No problem. We have games and things for the kids to do. We'll have your kids feeding the horses. I'll even give them a little hoe and they can be junior farmers. I have little straw hats from when my kids were little. Your kids will love it."

Tom looked at the clock. It was almost noon. "We all have each others' cell phones for last minute questions. Let's get out of here. See you guys tonight at my place. Thanks again, Jeff. We owe you big time." Tom had the feeling that this was the understatement of a lifetime.

"Hey, I'm just glad to have company," Jeff said. "This will be fun. I'll turn you city boys into farmers in no time." It was obvious that he was thrilled to be doing this; the mailroom guy was finally the center of attention.

Ben said very emphatically, "No one knows we're going out to your place, right?" He was asking Jeff and everyone else. "I'm serious. No one — I mean no one — outside your immediate family can know where we're going. I have a bad feeling about these protests. These people really hate us and there are tons of nut jobs out there." They all nodded.

As Tom was watching Ben, Brian, and Jeff leave his office, he had the strange sensation that they were all going into exile. But, of course that's not what we're doing, he thought to himself. It's just a few days on a farm, right?

Chapter 58

"You gonna eat that pickle?" II

(May 6)

The Team left Mrs. Nguyen's and went two doors down to Pow's. He checked his phone. There was that text from the unknown number.

"Shit!" Pow yelled. "Guys, guys, get over here. Looks like we have a mission."

Pow's excitement got the Team's full attention. "OK, looks like Grant needs us," Pow said. "Short version is that we need to get his family and bring them out to the cabin. He says we can stay out there as long as we want, and to bring lots of hardware. Bring all of it. All of it." They smiled at that.

They went over the new plan. It was getting dark, so things would be a little hairy, but things out there weren't yet total anarchy. They needed to do two things simultaneously: get Grant's family, and also get their stuff ready to go out to his cabin.

"It's not too bad out there," Pow said, referring to the conditions in Olympia. "I can go get Grant's family myself, and you guys can go back to your places and get your shit together. Let's meet back here in two hours."

They left and Pow got into his Hummer. He was carrying concealed, of course, and his AR was in the passenger seat. This would be a milk run. No big deal. His Hummer had plenty of room for the Matsons to put their stuff in.

Grant had given Pow the address in the text. He set out, keenly aware of the conditions out there. Things were still pretty calm; there were no sirens. It was like the police had either given up or were hunkered down and not driving around with their sirens on. There weren't many cars out. A couple more crazy asses sped by. No cops. Anywhere.

Pow slowly pulled into the entrance to the Cedars. There was an armed guard under the streetlight with a pump shotgun. That's it?

Wow, this place would be a easy to take over, he thought to himself.

Pow rolled his window down and showed both of his hands as if to say, "I'm unarmed" and waited for instructions. That Hummer wasn't a granny mobile, so maybe he'd get some more scrutiny. The guard put his shotgun up halfway and walked up to the driver's side. How predictable, he thought. These guys were out of their minds to have only one guard, and one who just walked up to the predictable side.

Pow took his "badge" from around his neck and put it out the window for the guard to see. He yelled, "I'm here to investigate the shooting last night." Grant had told him that in the text.

The guard saw the badge and lowered his shotgun. "Oh, hey, didn't expect to see you guys. You off duty or whatever?"

"Nope," Pow said, "we're all on duty now. All leave has been canceled. I'm a plainclothes. Where is the Matson house?" He avoided actually saying he was the police because he wasn't interested in committing any crimes, even if the police had their hands full and he would never go to jail for that.

The guard told him how to get there.

Pow decided to keep up the charade. "We've cleared Grant Matson in this. I just need to go interview his wife. Routine, you know." That would be a nice rumor to have the guard spread around. Pow was smart. More precisely, he had street smarts growing up in a rough Tacoma neighborhood.

Pow drove up to Grant's house. He had never seen it before. As close as the Team was, Grant had never invited them over. He said his wife would freak out. His house was pretty nice.

Pow rang the doorbell. It took a while for anyone to answer, even though the lights were on inside. The porch light came on. A very attractive professional-looking woman came to the door. She wouldn't open it.

Pow showed her the badge through the window in the door. He knew that word would spread like wildfire through the neighborhood that a "cop" had come, so he might as well have her think that, too. Besides, he needed her to open the door. He could apologize to her on the way out the cabin about having misled her.

He said through the door, "Sorry to bother you, Lisa."

She looked surprised. How did the police know her first name? This must be about Grant.

"Can I help you?" she asked.

He smiled, "Yes. This is about Grant. It's very good news."

Lisa let him in. She was surprised to see a six-foot tall Asian guy.

Pow paused and looked Lisa straight in the eye, smiled, and then asked, "You gonna eat that pickle?"

What? Why was a cop asking her about a pickle? Then Lisa remembered that this was Grant's first line to her back when they met.

"What?" Lisa asked. "I'm not sure I understand you." She couldn't believe what he had just said.

Pow smiled even bigger. "I am a friend of Grant's. We shoot together all the time, me and some other guys. Grant sent me a text." Pow held up the phone so she could see it. "He wants me and my guys to give you an armed escort to your cabin." Pow was bursting with pride. He felt fantastic that he and the Team could help Grant and his family reunite.

Lisa just stared at him.

Pow added, "He told me to use a code phrase about the pickle. Said you'd know it could only be from him."

That clever bastard, Lisa thought. Grant hadn't completely abandoned her and the kids. He was trying to reunite with them. And he had sent a cop with a Hummer to take them there. For the first time in two days she didn't hate him.

Lisa was still trying to process this amazing news. She just stood there staring at the cop offering an armed escort out to the cabin to be with Grant. Was this really happening?

The kids came downstairs, hearing that a visitor was there. Lisa motioned for them to go back into their rooms. She didn't want to alarm them.

Pow showed her the text. "Here's the text he wanted you to see."

Lisa could see it was from Manda's phone number. That's right, she remembered, yesterday Manda asked where her phone was. Grant took it. Why wouldn't he want to use his own phone, though?

She read the text:

"Lisa: I'm at the cabin. I'm fine. Things are great out here. I have 9 months of food. The gov't is collapsing. Seriously. I know from Jeanie. She told me top secret stuff. Things will get worse. You and the kids have to leave NOW. Leave. Leave. Leave. Pow is a Korean guy who is a friend. He has a team of guys who will provide an escort out here. You and the kids will be safe here. You won't in the city. I want to be with you. Please come out here. Love, G."

This was crazy, Lisa thought. She is just supposed to leave her house and get in a Hummer with a cop? There were some things on the news about things breaking down, but it wasn't the end of the world. The country was having some troubles like it did on 9/11, but it bounced back from that. This was nothing to overreact about.

Lisa wanted to go and be with Grant, but the idea of going wasn't...normal. Normal was the house, her job, the kids going to school tomorrow. Normal felt good. She wanted normal. Normal meant Grant being back and things being OK. Going off to the cabin would be admitting that things weren't normal, and that things were dangerous in Olympia.

"Sorry, but I don't think we need to go," Lisa said. "I appreciate you coming out here, but tell Grant we will stay here."

Pow was shocked. How could someone not want to go to a safe cabin?

"Really?" Pow blurted out. He was stunned. "I mean," he said pointing out toward the city center, "have you seen what's going on out there? Those looters will be back. Probably at night. You think they'll be OK with you guys shooting their homies? Are you kidding me?" Pow realized he was scaring her with reality. He reeled it back in. "I mean, I understand that it's a big thing to leave but, ma'am, you need to. It's not safe here."

Pow remembered the "badge" hanging around his neck and that Lisa thought he was a cop. He would use that. "Ma'am, I'm a professional and I'm telling you it's not safe here." He hated lying to her, but knew she'd thank him later.

Lisa stood there and thought. She knew it wasn't safe at her house, but it just seemed so weird to leave. Plus, if they left their house, it would probably get robbed and all her stuff would get broken. She couldn't just leave and let that happen.

But how could she stop robbers? Grant was gone. And she wouldn't touch that gun he left. Those things were dangerous. Ron and the other guards would prevent any robbers from coming in. And so would the police. After all, there was a police officer right now at her house; this proved to her that the police were still on patrol. The protests, or whatever those sirens were all about, would be over soon and things would get back to normal. Then Grant would figure out that he was just overreacting. He'd come home and things would be normal.

"No thank you," Lisa said. "We'll be fine."

Pow was speechless. He never even considered the idea that she wouldn't come. He figured she would view him as a hero.

He had to think of something to say since this wasn't going like he thought it would. "Well, OK," he said, "but Grant has Manda's phone so you can communicate with him that way." He got out a piece of paper and a pen. "Here is my cell phone number. When you change your mind, call or text me. Me and my team will be here, no matter how rough things are. Grant is a teammate and I'll risk my life for him. All of us on the Team will. We made a pact, ma'am."

That floored Lisa. Grant was on a "team"? What? A "pact"? This was all just too weird.

"OK, I'll call if I need you," Lisa said, "but I doubt I will. What I need is for Grant to come back home. Tell him that. His home is here, not out in the boonies somewhere."

Pow, the insurance salesman, felt like he was losing the biggest sale of his life. She and those kids would be dead in the city. "OK, ma'am," he said, not wanting to leave just in case he could figure out something to say to get her to come along. "But please call me when things get scary. They will." He reluctantly left.

Lisa closed the door and started crying again. This was all too much. Why couldn't Grant come back home? Why did he have to "win" by having her come out there? Why was he acting this way?

Manda came downstairs. "Mom, you should call that police officer. We need to go. Dad is right."

Lisa cried more when she heard Manda say, "Dad is right." Lisa was starting to realize this, too. But it was impossible to admit that they needed to go. She wanted "normal" back. She just wanted normal. And leaving for the cabin with an "armed escort" was not normal.

A few minutes later, Lisa heard gunfire in the distance. Then she heard a car horn honking and a car speed past her house. Then another. Was it another attack?

Manda went up to her room and came back down with the revolver Grant had left. Lisa was horrified that there was a gun in her house.

Manda said, "Mom, I'm going to have this with me. I don't care what you say. I have to do this." She sounded like an adult saying that.

Lisa didn't know how to respond. Her daughter was holding a gun. People might be attacking her neighborhood. Her husband was gone. A police officer had just been at the door offering them an armed escort out the cabin, and telling her that Grant was on the officer's "team" and had made a "pact." Lisa was getting dizzy. She needed to sit down.

After about twenty tense minutes, Sherri Spencer, Ron's wife, came to the door and said there had been a false alarm; it was only some shots a few subdivisions over. Lisa was relieved. See, nothing bad was happening to them, she thought.

Right now. But there were several more hours left before the sun came up. Lisa was praying for the sun to come up. It was the longest night. She was terrified.

Lisa took the police officer's phone number out of her pocket. She couldn't dial it. It was late and she didn't want to wake Grant up. She kept staring at the piece of paper.

"Call him," Manda said. Lisa didn't know she was standing there. "Call him, Mom."

"Go back to bed," Lisa said. This was not happening. This was not happening…

Chapter 59

Alone

(May 6)

Grant was on guard duty that night. He was alone; they had stopped the two-guard shifts because things were so peaceful out there. Besides, everyone was getting tired.

It was beautiful out there. It was May and the spring weather was fabulous. A clear night. But his mind was elsewhere.

He felt Manda's cell phone vibrate. It was Pow, who would be telling Grant when Lisa and the kids would be arriving. Grant couldn't wait to read that text.

The text said, "She wouldn't leave. Won't leave house. Said you need to come home. Sorry, man. I tried super hard. We're coming out soon. We can go back and get her if she calls."

He felt like someone kicked him in the stomach. He couldn't believe it.

Then it hit him: he was on his own. He no longer had a family. He was alone. He started crying and couldn't stop

His life was over. He had failed. He hadn't gotten his family through what he had known was coming for years. He had done all the preparing he could, but he still lost because his family wouldn't make it. He'd rather be dead than have them go through what was ahead of them. How could this be? He had plenty of food and a safe place, but no family to share it with. What good was that?

You'll see. They will be fine. Have faith.

Was that just wishful thinking? The outside thought had not been wrong so far. It had told him to prepare when the rest of the world continued to live obliviously. It told him a crisis was coming even when that seemed preposterous.

Grant remembered that survivors of various disasters always said the same thing: once you quit trying to live, you will die. You have to believe that you'll make it. And making it was not just that Grant himself lived; it meant Grant and his family surviving. So he decided that he would find a way to get his family. They would come out to the cabin. He would figure out a way.

He sat there the rest of the night. Alone. He immersed himself in constructive thoughts. How to guard the cabins. How to get food. How to introduce himself to other neighbors so they could start a bigger and bigger common defense and food sharing system. It didn't take long before he fell asleep.

Chapter 60

Power

(May 6)

"It's time to go," Tony, Menlow's chief of staff, said to Jeanie. She picked up her single suitcase and followed him.

Tony and Jeanie got Menlow and met Trooper Vasquez. They went to the parking garage, which was nearly empty. An unmarked police car pulled up, and the uniformed trooper opened the doors and trunk. Vasquez loaded the suitcases, said something to the driver, and motioned for them to get in the car. Tony took the front passenger seat so it was the Menlow and Jeanie in the back seat. It felt surreal.

Everyone was silent for the first few minutes. They saw the capitol campus go by out their window. They were heading onto the freeway, to who knows where.

Menlow finally broke the silence. "You know, Jeanie, the Governor called me and said that the State Legislature will be on recess for the foreseeable future. There are things going on in D.C. that would boggle your mind, too."

Jeanie was stunned. Menlow just stared out the window.

"Do you know what 'black bagging' is?" He asked Jeanie.

"No," she said.

"It's when the government grabs someone," Menlow said, "puts a black bag over their head, and takes them away to prison, or torture, or death. It's what all the teabaggers are worried about and it's what's sparking this thing off," he said. "You know, with the checkpoints we've set up?"

Jeanie was thoroughly confused. Menlow seemed to be out there in space.

"It's been out there for quite some time," Menlow said, "that Homeland Security thought the biggest terrorist threat was returning vets, conservatives, libertarians, Ron Paul types. You know."

Jeanie had been to the Homeland Security trainings at the State Auditor's Office about what to look out for. The "terrorists" in the training materials were always "militia types." Never Arabs. But Jeanie was still confused. Maybe Menlow had lost it.

"Well, these vets and teabaggers," Menlow said, still staring out the window, "have been getting stopped the past couple of days at the check points. They don't know if it's just a traffic stop or if they'll be 'black bagged.' The Feds can do that, you know? To 'belligerents' or 'enemy combatants' or whatever…" Menlow just trailed off as he looked out the window.

Jeanie had heard about that. It was the NDAA, the National Defense Authorization Act, but it was only supposed to be used on "terrorists."

"Yep," Menlow said, "so when a few of these teabaggers see the checkpoint, they think they're about to get 'black bagged.' So some of them decide they'll fight it out to the death rather than be taken away."

Menlow turned around to look at Jeanie and shrugged. "The sad part," he said to her, "is that the checkpoints weren't to pick up teabaggers but, now that cops are getting killed left and right, it's turned into that."

Menlow turned away from Jeanie and stared out the window again. "A self-fulfilling prophecy," he said. "A sad and horrible self-fulfilling prophecy."

Menlow looked out the window at the people on the street. Those poor folks had no idea what was coming. He felt sorry for them, but he was glad he was in the back of a police car going to someplace safe. He focused back on his brief phone call with the Governor.

"The Governor is signing a bunch of executive orders," Menlow said. "Emergency powers. They had a plan for this worked out some time ago, but no one thought they'd ever have to carry it out."

Menlow paused and kept staring out the window. Finally, he said, "You know…the cycle is broken. The political cycle. Where the Ds spend a bunch of tax money and then some Rs get elected. Then Ds win, then Rs do, all the while, each side is spending more and more. Maybe at different rates, but spending more. Well, that's over now."

Menlow paused and looked out the window some more. Those poor bastards out there walking around, Menlow thought. They have no idea.

"Politics is over," Menlow said as he turned to look Jeanie in the eye. "This can't be fixed with elections. That's a big thing for a politician to admit," he said with a chuckle. He turned away from Jeanie and looked back out the window.

"We can't restore order with politics," Menlow said with a sigh. "Politics? That's how we got here. It will take something bigger than politics to get things stabilized. Power. That's what it will take. Power." He kept staring out the window.

Everyone was silent.

Menlow continued, "The Feds are doing the same stuff. Emergency powers. Some scary stuff. You know the old line, 'Never let a good crisis go to waste.' They're not. They're going to announce a new civilian law enforcement auxiliary called the 'Freedom Corps.' This is like 9/11 times a hundred."

More silence. Now they were getting on the freeway. Menlow said, "Oh, did I mention that the Southern states are basically seceding? Yep. Everyone's wondering what the military will do. I wonder about our National Guard in this state. How many will be willing to carry out some of these new powers? Then again, it's the only way to stop the chaos." Menlow wouldn't admit it out loud, but he was thinking it: now is precisely the time the state needed a law-and-order Republican governor. He smiled. Power.

Chapter 61

Weenie Uprising

(May 6)

Nancy Ringman had been sent home that morning like all other state employees at the capitol. She couldn't believe how the state and Feds were letting these right-wing hateful Tea Partiers push everyone around. She knew that the right was responsible for all the terrorism. The corporate media was saying it was the "Red Brigade," but Nancy knew it was those gun-toting right-wingers. They were masquerading as "welfare protestors" and destroying the city. She hated them.

The rumor mill at her office had already described the new "Freedom Corps." That sounded like a good idea. It would give people like her, leaders and people traditionally excluded from the "good ole' boy" system, a chance to help the state restore order. She couldn't wait to join. She would lead the Freedom Corps in her neighborhood, of course.

That reminded her. The "good ole' boys" were running wild in her own neighborhood. Ron and Len were turning the Cedars into an armed camp. And Grant Matson had murdered those kids, which was completely unnecessary. Gunfire in a residential area! What were those men thinking?

Nancy hated having to see men with guns every time she drove in and out of the subdivision. Macho. That's all it was. Some men trying to be macho. She felt the neighborhood gravitating toward them and their guns. She could feel she was losing power.

There was a meeting of the neighborhood association planned for that evening. She would make a stand against the testosterone. If she didn't do it now, everyone would think guns were the answer to all of this.

When Nancy arrived, she called the meeting to order. "Everyone is so thankful for Ron and Len and the other volunteers, but I have a concern," she said. "It seems the more guns we have out, the more they get used. Grant, who has apparently abandoned his family, killed three kids and wounded four more. It was horrible. And it wouldn't have happened without a macho hothead like that deciding to spray the neighborhood with automatic weapons. We need a better way to stay safe because, quite honestly, I don't feel safe with all of these guns around."

"I suggest that we have people out observing, but that we call the police if we need help," she said. "The police are trained professionals." That resonated with the audience. They had been told their whole lives that life was complicated and to leave things up to the experts.

It didn't resonate with everyone, though.

Ron asked, "Have you seen a cop lately? One of these 'trained professionals' we are supposed to rely on?"

Someone said, "One came out to interview Lisa Taylor."

"OK, has anyone seen any cops out preventing crimes instead of writing reports about killings that have already happened?" Ron asked. He was not using an angry voice; he was speaking very calmly.

Nancy knew who her enemy was.

"Ron, what about the shooting the other night in Becker Acres?" she asked in a condescending voice, which was the only tone she seemed to have, other than mock sweetness. "There were bullets flying toward us. Is that safe?"

"It's safer than a pack of thugs with rifles and clubs trying to kill you," Ron said. "I know a little something about that. Remember? I was fighting them off while you slept." Ron was pissed that he was even having to make this obvious point.

After a couple of days of sleep deprivation and being attacked by a gang of armed thugs, his usual accountant calm and politeness was gone. Everyone was getting frayed. Emotions were raw.

"I just don't feel safe with all these guns around," Nancy repeated, making it obvious that her argument was simply that she didn't feel safe around guns. That was it. No plan for security, just her feelings.

Ron blew up. "I don't give a damn about your phobias! I care about preventing vicious criminals from attacking my family and even yours. What the hell is the matter with you?" A few people clapped. Nancy knew that she was losing a political fight.

Her emotions were raw, too. After several days of watching those government-hating knuckle dragging Tea Party people shut everything down, she'd had enough. She was going to do something about it.

"Ron, we don't need your macho testosterone," she said with her teeth clenched. "We need a civilized way to help the police do their job. I propose that we discontinue the armed camp approach and form a local chapter of the Freedom Corps."

No one said anything.

Nancy realized that they hadn't yet heard of the Freedom Corps, since they weren't government insiders like her. She felt so powerful.

"Freedom Corps," she explained, "will be announced soon to the general public." She loved the hint that only important people like her knew about this. "It's a civilian law enforcement auxiliary. We will work with law enforcement to help them while they have other things to look after. You will hear about it on the news soon. Judy, you're in law enforcement, what do you think about this?"

Nancy called on Judy Kilmer, an administrative law judge living on Grant's cul-de-sac. Nancy had rehearsed this with Judy beforehand. Judy was a supporter.

Judy decided little administrative cases like unemployment benefit appeals, environmental permit fines, and paperwork violations for people subject to state licensing. "Law enforcement" was an absurd stretch. But, Nancy knew most people in the neighborhood worked for and, to varying degrees, revered government, so a "judge" would have lots of credibility.

"Well," Judy said, "I know that it's very important to have an orderly system for protection. Just shooting people and running away isn't that. You need to have systems in place to help law enforcement do its job. It's more about collecting and preserving evidence than just killing."

Ron couldn't believe what he was hearing. He yelled, "Collecting and preserving evidence after what?" He threw his hands up in the air. "After a pack of shitbags has killed or raped my family? A lot of good evidence will do then. What's wrong with you?" Ron stormed out of the room.

Nancy gave Ron a "tsk, tsk" facial expression and rolled her eyes. "See, this is that kind of testosterone outburst that, coupled with guns, leads to violence," she scolded.

The crowd of neighborhood people, almost all of whom were government workers who respected Nancy and Judy's high positions, appeared to be thinking about this. It was likely that they understood the logic and even the emotion of Ron's side, but wanted Nancy's approach to work. "Normal" meant no longer seeing armed men at the entrance to the neighborhood. Everyone wanted normal back. The group was silent for a minute or so. Nancy could sense that she was winning.

"Let's meet back here tomorrow night at the same time," Nancy said, which was also part of her rehearsed plan. "That will give everyone a chance to think this over."

And it would give Nancy time to visit each neighbor and lobby them. She wanted to see Lisa Taylor, in particular. She hated the Matsons, especially Grant who got her fired from the State Auditor's Office. If Grant was a big baby and had run from the police, Nancy at least wanted to get in Lisa's face and tell her what a horrible person her husband was.

Chapter 62

Sheepdogs on Patrol

(May 6)

Pow's plan was blown. He had assumed he'd help Grant's family pack and then take them back to his place, meet up with the Team, and go out to Grant's cabin that night. He didn't want to leave for the cabin without Grant's family. But, he didn't want to stay in the city. He wasn't sure the guys would want to, either. He was trying to figure out what to do. He was the leader, but it was pretty close to a democracy. He couldn't suggest they do something unpopular. But he didn't want to leave Lisa and kids in danger.

Driving back to his place, Pow could see that things were getting worse. No normal people were out on the streets. There were packs of questionable people walking the streets. There were still no cops. There were still no sirens. At first, Pow thought this was a good sign. Then he realized it wasn't; the cops were giving up, retreating to strongholds somewhere else, or were running out of the gas that was required to run their cars.

People were starting to realize they were on their own. Most were shocked, but a few, the criminals and the criminal wannabes, were starting to realize the opportunities that existed until law enforcement restored order. If they ever did.

Pow got back to his house earlier than the two hours he'd told the guys. They weren't there yet. He pulled into his neighborhood. At the entrance was Clay Porter, a retired Army guy who lived a few streets away. He was in his truck under the streetlight. Pow slowed down and rolled down his window.

"Hey, Clay, what's up?" He asked.

"Oh, hey, Pow," Clay said, "glad to see you. Shit's hitting the fan, that's what's up. We need to talk."

Pow knew that he was about to be asked to help the neighborhood. "Sure. Let's talk," he said.

"We need a neighborhood patrol," Clay said. "We need you

and those guys over at your house all the time. I've got a dozen or so vets and some young guys. We need a guard rotation. We also need to get food and gas, which means going out on runs. They will get more and more dangerous as this continues. You in?"

"Sure," Pow said without even thinking, just like he did with Mrs. Nguyen. Pow was a sheepdog. He helped people. Once his neighborhood was squared away, he and the Team could bug out to Grant's. It would give the guys something to do while he waited to hear from Grant's wife. There was a risk that by waiting to go to the cabin things would get so bad in the city that they couldn't make it out, but that risk was mainly for unarmed and untrained people. Not the Team. That seemed somewhat cocky to Pow, but he felt this was the right decision. He really wanted to give Grant's wife some time to decide that she wanted to go to the cabin, after all. He wanted to kill some time, even when time was precious.

"My guys are coming in about an hour," Pow said. "We'll come over to your place after that." Pow didn't want to have Clay over to his place with all the valuable guns and cases of ammo visible. Clay was a good guy, but Pow didn't feel comfortable advertising his goods.

Pow went back to his house and looked over all this stuff. He was so reassured to have it. They had some serious firepower.

One by one, the guys were rolling in. Pow knew they would want to get out to the cabin right away. This neighborhood patrol with Clay was delaying that. He told each one the new plan as they arrived, instead of telling the whole group. He could convince one guy at a time easier than convincing the whole group. In the end, all of them were OK with spending a couple days patrolling Pow's neighborhood. It would be fun; this is what the Team lived for.

They went over to Clay's with concealed pistols and met the other men in the neighborhood. They were a pretty solid bunch of guys. Not nearly as well armed as the Team, but they had plenty of decent hunting weapons and good pistols. Two guys even said they had ARs. Many of the neighborhood guys had good military experience, but they hadn't been to a shooting range almost every other weekend like the Team had. Regardless, they were a very good group, well armed and decently trained.

With Pow and Clay leading, and given the high percentage of veterans, it didn't take long to get a guard system and shift schedule down. They would guard the entrance with at least one guy with an AR. The military guys all knew how to operate one so there was always someone ready to use one. One truck would patrol around. One or two trucks with well-armed men would go out and get food and gas for residents. The elderly and families with young kids would get first dibs on the supply runs. Armed supply runs were feeling "normal" for the Team. They'd been doing that a lot lately.

In a matter of two days, the world had totally changed. At least, for people like the Team; people who had the right mindset. The rest of the world was catching up to them, slowly realizing how different things had become.

But, not all were making the adjustment. Pow watched one guy in the neighborhood, a recently retired guy, washing his '69 Mustang over and over again. Pow went over to talk to him and all the guy could talk about was all the things he'd done in that Mustang. He was almost in a trance. He wasn't thinking about getting food or gas or the crime all around them. He just mumbled about that car and kept washing it. Pow walked away and the man didn't even notice. Pow knew that he wasn't going to make it through this. He didn't want to. He wanted to be riding in that Mustang. He wanted "normal" back, and would die trying.

Chapter 63

POI

(May 6)

The ride to the "secure location" should have been pretty short, but it took three hours. Jeanie knew where they were going; it wasn't a mystery. They would go the fifteen miles or so north on I-5 to the Washington National Guard Headquarters at the giant Army and Air Force base called Joint Base Lewis McChord, or JBLM as everyone called it.

Sure enough. That's where they were going. Traffic was extremely heavy. I-5 was the main interstate up and down Washington State. The Seattle metropolitan area stretched from Olympia in the south up I-5 about a hundred miles to Marysville in the north. The whole metro area straddled I-5.

Many other people were going places, too, and I-5 was how to get there. The roads were tightly designed to accommodate normal loads. If just five percent more cars than normal were on the road, traffic would jam up, especially when cars were stalled out. Jeanie saw that many were; she presumed they were out of gas. When that happened, people would honk and get furious. Eventually, they would push the car over to the shoulder. People were standing around their disabled cars on the side of the road. Jeanie knew that bad things were probably going to happen to those people.

I-5 was a parking lot. There was no movement most of the time. Emergency vehicles were using the left lane. After a while, non-emergency vehicles starting driving in that lane, too, following the emergency vehicles just to get by the traffic jams. That was a misdemeanor; but no one was writing tickets.

The car Jeanie was in would drive in the left lane and on the shoulder when it wasn't blocked. Her car had cop lights in the grill, and the trooper driving was using them.

Menlow just looked out the window. Since they were stopped most of the time, he could look into the windows of cars stopped next to his and see their faces. He saw families screaming at each other. He saw terrified faces. He saw kids crying. And, Menlow realized, the people in these cars were just the 1% who realized they needed to get out of the cities before it really got bad. What about the 99% still sitting in their homes awaiting instructions from the authorities?

As Menlow looked at all the people stuck in traffic trying to flee, he thought about all the problems that needed to be solved. Gas would need to be distributed. Food, too. The people on the side of road with disabled vehicles would need places to stay. People would need medical care. He smiled inside.

This meant government would need to do those things. Need. Need. People would depend on government for their very lives, and he was going to be running the government. Once he got elected, of course, but with the Governor not running for re-election and the state craving a Republican to fix things, he'd be in for sure. He would be the greatest governor in state history. He allowed himself to actually smile. He felt warm inside.

Finally, they took the exit for JBLM. Traffic was backed up around Ft. Lewis. There were soldiers with rifles checking IDs. They were turning people away. It took forever to get past the gate, but Jeanie's car got right through. The guards radioed in when the trooper used a code word. They were on a list of expected guests.

They went to a nondescript building. It had very big radio antennas on it. There were soldiers and police everywhere. Jeanie wasn't used to being around people with guns, especially rifles. Everyone looked so serious. And scared. And tired.

"You can work from here until your quarters are ready," said a female soldier as she showed Jeanie, Menlow, and Tony a small conference room.

Work? Doing what? Auditing state agencies? It was pretty apparent they wouldn't be doing their old jobs. They were here because Menlow was "five heartbeats" away from being the governor. No one really thought the first five wouldn't be able to be the governor; it was probably just some dusty Cold War-era continuity of government plan that said the Auditor needed to be at the National Guard headquarters if something happened. And it had happened.

They just sat there. Jeanie looked at her watch. It was 3:22 p.m. They weren't talking; they were just waiting to be told what to do. After a while, the female soldier said, "Come with me, please," and motioned for them to follow her. They went down a few hallways into a bigger conference room which had many of the same people who were usually at the state agency leadership briefings. There was Jason from the Governor's Office who had briefed them that morning.

"Hi," Jason said as Jeanie, Tony, and Menlow walked in. As they were taking their seats, Jason continued with what he had been saying to the rest of the people in the room.

"Here's what's going on," he said. "The Governor declared a military emergency a few hours ago. This means that our continuity of government plan goes into effect. That's why you're here, Mr. Auditor. You won't be doing your normal job until this is over, which hopefully will be soon. We will ask you and your staff to work with the Governor's Office to help with the relief efforts."

Menlow nodded. He loved this.

"The National Guard has been activated, of course," Jason said. "They are reporting in for duty as soon as they can get to their duty stations. Only a few people are able to come in, though. The police are on full alert. Oh, by the way, the capitol campus has been evacuated and protestors have pretty much trashed the place. Technically, the new seat of government is right here," Jason said as he waved his hands around the conference room.

"We are working closely with federal authorities to start rounding up the people responsible for this," Jason said. "There are some suspected terrorists we've, or rather the federal authorities, have been watching in our state. They're getting them. There are also some radical political groups to watch. We are assisting them with the round ups."

"What radical political groups?" Menlow asked.

"Some left-wing terrorist groups. Sympathizers with the Red Brigades," Jason said. "Oh, and some Tea Party and Oath Keeper militia types. Lots of those. Actually, most of them are teabaggers."

Jason continued, "We have started something called 'POIs.' That stands for 'Persons of Interest.' They are people who are not suspected of a crime per se, but are people we want to talk to. Right-wing political types, mostly. In fact, Ms. Thompson, we'd like you to work on getting the POI list out to the media."

"Sure," Jeanie said. This was so exciting.

Jason handed her a scrap of paper. "Here is a password to our system. You'll see the POI list there and can get started formulating a message."

Jeanie nodded. Wow. This was amazing.

"I need to take the Auditor and his Chief of Staff to go meet with the others in the line of succession," Jason said. He took them with him. There was Jeanie in the big conference room with a bunch of other civilians and some military people. OK, time to get to work.

Jeanie logged on and opened the POI file. It was very interesting to see who was on that list. She didn't recognize any names, of course, until one jumped out at her on the screen.

"Matson, Grant." Near his name was "Foster, Tom," "Trenton, Benjamin," and "Jenkins, Brian." The next column said "Wash. Assn. of Business" and "'Rebel Radio." What the hell were WAB people doing on a "Persons of Interest" list?

She suddenly felt like she might be on the POI. She searched for her name. Nothing. She wasn't on there. She started panicking. The government was going to try to arrest her friends. There must be some mistake.

She wondered about her boyfriend, Jim. He was really conservative and had mentioned to friends that he thought the people would start a revolution soon. She hadn't thought about him much today. There had been too much excitement. He was off on Guard duty and was probably fine. He was surrounded by many well armed men. He would be busy doing his computer job for the Guard. She missed him. It would be so great to be home and with him if all of this wasn't happening. But it was and she had a job to do. She tried to do it. But she couldn't think. Her boyfriend was away from her, possibly in danger, and she was being asked to help the government round up her friends.

A female plainclothes cop came over to her. "Are you Thompson, the one working on getting the POI list out?" She asked Jeanie.

"Yes," Jeanie said.

"I'm Sergeant Winslow, WSP," which meant Washington State Patrol. She looked at Jeanie's screen and saw the POI list was there. "Pretty interesting list of characters, huh?"

"Yeah," Jeanie said. "So how did you create this?"

"There were some troubling groups out there," Winslow said. "As things got bad with the economy and the political situation became more heated, these groups got more vocal. We used some informants for the secretive ones. For the vocal ones, we used Facebook and similar social media."

"Facebook?" Jeanie said.

"Oh, yeah," Winslow said. "When we found one person of interest, we'd look and see who his or her friends were on Facebook or other social media. We'd check the 'mutual friends' thing and, poof, we had a really good start to the list. And all their contact information was there. That's how most of these people got on the list. Facebook. It's a wonderful tool for us." She was smiling.

Oh crap. Jeanie started to wonder if she was a Facebook friend with any of the WAB people? No. She remembered that Menlow had asked her to unfriend them after he decided to run for governor. Whew.

"OK," Jeanie said, trying to focus on doing her job so she didn't look suspicious. "How do you want to get these names out to the media? Is the internet still working for the outside world?" she asked. They talked about how to the get the list out. The whole time Jeanie wondered if she was betraying Grant and the WAB guys, and who knows how many others of her conservative friends? But what was she going to do? Walk away? She was stuck on a military base surrounded by chaos. She had to stay. She had to do what was being asked. She told herself that she would do whatever she could to alert Grant without getting caught, herself.

Chapter 64

"Why are you hurting us?"

(May 7)

The morning after the first neighborhood meeting, Nancy Ringman was going around to each house trying to convince them that they needed to go along with her plan of looking to the police to secure the neighborhood. Nancy, of course, would coordinate all of it. She found many of the people receptive to her no-guns message. But they were questioning whether it really made sense not having an armed guard at the entrance to the Cedars subdivision.

By now, things were starting to get out of hand in Olympia. People were slowly starting to react to everything going on around them. Shelves in the grocery stores were getting bare. People were arguing in the parking lots and in lines. Some had even seen some fights. The lines at gas stations were becoming long and unruly. A rumor was spreading about someone in the neighborhood being shot during an argument at the gas station.

Nancy had one more cul-de-sac of households to talk to before the meeting later that night. It was Grant Matson's. She was getting tired. She hadn't slept a full night's sleep in two days; the excitement of these events kept her awake. She kept having the feeling that finally the good people like her would be in charge. Finally.

Nancy had run out of her anti-depressant, Prozac, when all of this started. "Anti-depressant" was a misleading term, she thought. The Prozac didn't make her feel less depressed; it helped her get along with people. It curbed what her doctor had politely termed her "aggressive impulses." Without it, she was mean. Really mean. She didn't have time to go get a prescription filled right now. There was a crisis and the neighborhood was depending on her for leadership.

Most of the people in the neighborhood were weaklings, Nancy thought. She needed a little extra meanness to lead people. It's called leadership, she told herself. She'd been mean her whole life and got a lot accomplished that way. People were wimps and needed someone to tell them what to do, she had found.

Nancy's phone vibrated. It was a text from Brenda, a former co-worker at the State Auditor's Office. It's first few letters were "POI!!!" It said that the Governor had created a list called "Persons of Interest" and had a link. The text went on: "Grant Matson is on it!!! He's POI!" She looked at the link, which loaded very slowly on her phone. She looked at the background on what the POI list was. Fabulous!

Grant Matson was officially a terrorist and a wanted man. Nancy was standing outside his house now. Finally, her government was doing something about people like Grant Matson. Finally, the cavalry had shown up. She was part of the solution to all of this chaos. She would help the effort by going to his house and finding out where he was hiding. She felt a surge of adrenaline. It felt so fabulous. She loved a good fight. Especially against a teabagger like Grant Matson and his obnoxiously pretty doctor wife.

Nancy felt so alive. She confidently walked right up to the Matson's door and knocked on it. It took a while for someone to answer. She saw Grant's wife looking through the blinds before she opened it.

"Yes," Lisa said. "Can I help you?" She vaguely recognized Nancy as someone from the neighborhood.

"Oh, yeah, you can help me," Nancy said in a very excited voice. Then Nancy yelled, "Where is that terrorist piece of shit husband of yours?"

Lisa was scared. What was this "terrorist" thing? And why was this woman yelling at her? Lisa could tell that Nancy was agitated like some of the people that came into the ER.

"What?" Lisa asked. "And please keep your voice down. My children are here," she said firmly.

"I don't give a shit who's home, except Grant Matson," Nancy yelled. "You need to tell me where he is. He's on the POI list and I'm here to find out where he's hiding."

"POI list?" Lisa said. "What's that?"

"The Governor's 'Persons of Interest' list," Nancy said with a sneer. Grant's pretty little wife wasn't nearly as well informed as Nancy was. "It's a wanted list of terrorists like your right-wing asshole husband. That's what. So where is he, bitch?"

Lisa couldn't believe someone was talking to her that way. "What did you just call me?"

"Bitch," Nancy said, flatly. "Where is Grant Matson?" Nancy paused for effect, "bitch." She loved this. She had hated Grant Matson for so long, and now she could finally get even.

Lisa turned from being shocked to furious. She tried to slam the door in Nancy's face, but Nancy had put her foot in the door.

Nancy screamed, "Nice try, bitch. Let me in right now!"

The kids came out of their rooms and were at the top of the stairs, watching the commotion at the front door. Manda wanted to help. She grabbed Cole by the hand and they ran downstairs to help their mom against this crazy lady at the front door.

Lisa and Nancy struggled with the door. Finally Nancy, in a burst of adrenaline strength, pushed the door open and knocked Lisa down.

Thirteen year old autistic Cole lunged at Nancy. She pushed him back and knocked him to the ground hard. Really hard.

Cole hit the ground and cried out, "Why are you hurting us?"

Those words rang out. Why are you hurting us?

That did it for Lisa. Instantly, everything became clear. This was a war. No one hurts my kids, especially my innocent little Cole, she thought. Who was this violent bitch trying to break into her house? Lisa realized that she was in a fight. Not just with Nancy but with all of them. Things were not normal. People like Nancy had gone insane and were trying to hurt her and her family. Nancy hated Grant for some political reasons that were stupid. Instead of thinking "this can't be happening," right at that instant, Lisa realized it *was* happening, and she needed to take care of her family or something unthinkable would happen.

She jumped toward Nancy. Lisa was a runner and in great shape. She could take this fat baby boomer bitch who hurt Cole. She planted her shoulder in Nancy's chest and knocked her down, then she started punching Nancy. Lisa felt her fists starting to hurt; she was totally out of control. She was fighting for her kids. She was beating the shit out of the crazy woman who was trying to break into their house.

Manda ran upstairs to get her revolver. She had to do something to help. She got the gun case out of her closet and opened the combination lock. She ran down the stairs with the gun in her hand.

By the time Manda got halfway down the stairs, she could see her mom had the crazy woman pinned to the ground and was punching her in the face. Manda thought her mom might kill the woman. Manda just watched, ready to shoot the woman if she got up. She saw Cole lying on the ground crying near the door. Manda grabbed him and took him into the nearby bathroom to keep him safe. Things were happening so fast. Manda went back to the entryway and saw her mom was standing over the woman. Her mom's hands were bleeding and she was breathing heavy.

Lisa caught her breath and yelled, "Get out of my house, bitch!" She kicked Nancy. "Get out. If you come back, I'll kick your ass again. Never hurt my son. Never. Get out before I get my gun."

Nancy got up. She was afraid of getting shot. She ran out of the house. Those Matsons were crazy. Violent. No wonder he was a terrorist on the POI list. Nancy ran down the driveway and across the street to the Spencer's house. She was yelling for someone to call 911. Sherri Spencer came out to see what was wrong. Nancy was bloodied and bruised, and told Sherri that Lisa Matson had beaten her. Sherri ran over to the Matsons.

Sherri saw Lisa, with blood on her hands, and yelled, "What's going on? Are you OK?"

Lisa was catching her breath. "Nancy Ringman tried to break into my house. She hurt Cole. She's crazy. She started hitting me. I fought back. She's crazy."

This was too much for Sherri. Her neighbors, two professional women, were fist fighting each other? That made no sense.

Lisa realized that she might have committed a crime. Not really, since it was self defense, but she realized that Nancy would claim that Lisa attacked her with a sword or something nuts like that.

Lisa yelled to Sherri, "Watch out. Nancy is crazy. Go protect your kids. She's got something wrong with her. Go! Now." Sherri ran back home.

Lisa heard Cole crying in the bathroom and ran in there to comfort him. "Don't worry, lil' guy, the bad lady is gone. She won't be back."

Cole looked at her and asked again, "Why are they hurting us?" That struck Lisa. Why are they hurting us? Why? Lisa wondered that herself. Why was a neighbor coming over to scream and fight and try to arrest her husband? Things were not normal.

Lisa knew what she had to do. She went downstairs and found that scrap of paper with the Korean cop's phone number on it. They needed to get out of here. Things were crazy. There would be more Nancys and probably police now that Grant was on some terrorist list. There was no more "normal."

Chapter 65

Milk Run Chaos

(May 7)

That morning, Pow was going out on a "milk run," as they called it. That's where they would escort some neighborhood people to the grocery store and the gas station. Things were still semi-civil in town. There was violence, but a very small percentage of people were engaged in it. Most were just trying to get some food and gas and get back home in one piece. And most were doing so successfully.

Many grocery stores and gas stations had a police car at the entrance, although there wasn't always a cop to go with the car. Sometimes, the cops parked their car at a store and walked over to another one to double their coverage. There were occasional sirens, which just added to the scariness because it reminded people how the sirens went constantly a few days ago and now were largely silent. There was a definite sense that the police could not possibly control things anymore. But, most people still believed they could, despite the evidence they were seeing with their own eyes. Decades of thinking the police would always be there prevented people from evaluating the facts before their eyes.

At the stores, people were arguing and occasionally throwing punches to get the last of some kind of food or a place in the gas line. That would have been an amazing event in peacetime, but now was common. Wes and Scotty watched as a woman drew a revolver at a large man in the parking lot of the grocery store. By the time they could get over to where she was, the guy took off.

Overall, the Team was very surprised that things had not devolved into full-scale warfare. It amazed them that the stores were still open and selling things. The shelves were getting bare, prices were much higher, and the stores were only taking cash. Most people had come to realize that something bad was happening and that they better stock up for a few days. But they didn't think this was the end of the world.

That morning, the rumor went around that the banks had closed and the ATMs were running out of cash. Bobby confirmed this when he was on the milk run. It made sense that the banks and ATMs would be closed. Armored cars full of money to restock them weren't exactly driving around right now. Cash, like everything else, was supplied on a just-in-time inventory basis. And, with the internet down frequently, credit and debit cards weren't working. No stores would take checks. Cash was it. And it was virtually gone.

This was a turning point. People would freak out when, finally, after looking all over town for some product they desperately needed, the store wouldn't take their credit or debit card and they had no cash. They would yell, sometimes hit people, and occasionally pull out a gun. But no one on the Team had heard a gunshot yet.

Some of the people from Pow's neighborhood went to the stores on their own, without the escort Pow and Clay had organized. Most would bring a handgun with them.

It was amazing how many guns were coming out of the woodwork. Old .38 Specials and grandpa's .45 from the war were being dusted off from sock drawers and being tucked into belts. People were carrying guns even if they didn't have a concealed weapons permit. That law now seemed a quaint little rule from the past. Now, with what was going on, requiring a concealed weapons permit seemed like requiring a permit to breathe.

Some people in Pow's neighborhood went to the store without a gun the day before. It didn't turn out so well for two of them, an older man and wife, the Terrytons. They were robbed on their way there. Some young thugs in a pickup truck pulled up beside them at the intersection, jumped out, and forced their way into the Terrytons' car. The thugs pulled the Terrytons out of their car, beat them, took their money and jewelry, and stole their car. This happened in broad daylight. The Terrytons were beaten unconscious and laying in the intersection for a while until some people pulled them onto the sidewalk. A bystander tried to perform first aid, but there were no ambulances or police cars. After a while, the bystander had to get to the store herself before it got dark, so she reluctantly left them there. The Terrytons died on a sidewalk as several hundred people drove by.

Chapter 66

Bugging Out of the Cedars

(May 7)

It was mid-afternoon. Pow was taking a break at his house after escorting two single moms on their trip to the grocery store. He was so tired; it was exhausting constantly being on guard. It was a different kind of tired than just staying up late. It was draining.

His cell phone vibrated. It was a text from a number he didn't recognize. It said: "Grant's wife here. We want to go. Can you still take us? Please. Urgent."

Pow jumped up and yelled. Awesome. The Team could do their best deed yet: delivering Grant's family to him. And having a great place out in the country to stay and continue their sheepdogging. And they would be out of the city where things were breaking down by the hour.

Pow tried calling Lisa. The call went through, although voice service had become more and more spotty. A woman answered.

"Mrs. Matson, this is Bill Kung here," Pow said.

"Are you coming for us?" Lisa asked. She sounded desperate.

"Yes, ma'am," Pow said. "That's the plan. I need to know when you'll be ready."

"It will take a few hours," Lisa said, "I have to make sure the kids have all their stuff." Lisa had the packing list down from years of getting ready for vacations. That's what this would be, she told herself. A week or two away from the house and then things would be normal. Except that thing about Grant being a terrorist. That would get cleared up. He was a lawyer. He'd tell a judge he wasn't a terrorist and things would work out.

Pow looked at his watch. It was 2:45 p.m. It would be dark in six hours. It was May and sunset was very late in Washington State. He didn't want to go out at night, which was when the bad guys were starting to come out in full force. They slept during the day.

"Could you be ready in two hours?" Pow asked. The Team was

already at his house with all their stuff. In fact, they were fully packed and ready to go. Full magazines and full gas tanks. They were just waiting for this call. They could be ready to roll out in no time.

"Oh, I could," Lisa said. "But my parents need to come, too. It will take them longer."

Parents? What?

"Do they live around here?" Pow asked. They better, he thought. He wasn't going into Seattle for anything.

"Yeah, they're about two miles from me," Lisa said. "I couldn't go without them."

Mission creep. That's the term for when a mission starts to expand beyond what made sense in the first place. Pow could see this was happening to the relatively simple job of picking up Grant's family and going out to the cabin. But he knew that things weren't so bad that waiting a little while longer and taking more people out to the cabin was a life-and-death situation.

"Where, exactly, do they live?" he asked.

Lisa told him. It was a good neighborhood so it should be fairly safe. Probably.

"OK," Pow said. He'd been helping people for days now. No reason to stop doing it now. "When can they be ready?"

"I'd say three hours," she said, which was a complete guess because she hadn't even talked to them about coming. She wanted to see if the Korean cop could still escort them out there before she brought up the topic of leaving with her parents.

"OK," Pow said. "They need to be ready, absolutely ready, to go at 6:00. I'll be at your house at 5:30. I'm bringing three other trucks of guys so we need to go right then. No waiting around."

Three trucks of guys? Lisa had only met one guy, the cop who came to her door.

"Who will be in the three trucks and who are the guys?" Lisa asked.

"The Team," Pow said proudly. "We have been training with Grant for over a year. These guys, Wes, Scotty, and Bobby, are like me. We're very well armed. Grant told me last summer that we could come out to the cabin if the shit hit the…if things got dangerous in town. He said that having us out there was part of his plan, so that you and the kids would be 'well taken care of.' He said we could stay at one of the cabins out there, the yellow one owned by the guy from California."

Lisa decided that she needed to test this claim that Grant had taken this man out to the cabin and wanted them to come out. She didn't want to get into a truck with someone who wasn't helping Grant. "Describe the cabin to me," she said.

Pow described it perfectly, including the neighbors. "Their names begin with a 'C' and an 'M.'" The Colsons and the Morrells, Lisa thought.

Well, his description of the place and the names of the neighbors were right, she thought. Grant had texted her from Manda's phone and said she should go out to the cabin with the Pow guy, who was apparently a cop. Plus the Korean man used that same phrase Grant had, that they would be "well taken care of." So these guys must be part of Grant's plan.

Wow, Lisa thought. Grant had thought of everything and done all this behind her back. At first she was mad that he done all this secretly. Then she realized how lucky she was to have a husband who did all this. And how lucky she was to have a guy on the phone who was willing to risk his life and his friends' to take her and her family to safety. This was all too incredible to believe. But so was having Nancy Ringman hurting Cole. And all those sirens she had been hearing for days that were now quiet. And the men with guns at the neighborhood entrance. And now getting picked up by some armed strangers Grant had been "training" with.

But this was real, Lisa thought. Yes, this was happening. They needed to get out of here. Nancy Ringman's attack on them had made that obvious. OK, Lisa thought, it's time to get practical and get to safety.

"I'll be driving my Tahoe," Lisa said. "That will work, right?"

"Sure," Pow said. "You'll need something to take your things in. My guys have all their stuff in their rigs so we don't have much extra room. Besides, you'll want to have your car when things get better in a few days and you can drive back home," Pow said, knowing that things wouldn't get better that quickly, but wanting to make her think otherwise. "We will put your car in the middle of the convoy. You'll have some firepower in front of you and behind you. You'll be very safe."

"My parents will be in their car," Lisa said. "That will be OK?"

"Sure," Pow said. "Same thing. They'll be in the middle of the convoy."

"OK. I'll get them ready," Lisa said. "Come at 5:30. Thanks again… I'm sorry. What was your name?" Lisa asked.

"Pow," he said. "You can call me Pow."

"OK, Pow," she said. "See you at 5:30." Lisa hung up. She had to call her parents now. She didn't know if they would understand. She called them. The cell lines were busy. She tried the landline. It was working. Her dad answered.

"Dad," Lisa said, "I need you to listen to me. The kids and me, and hopefully you and Mom, are going out to the cabin. Grant is out there. He's safe. It's safe there. He has food out there and guns. He has been preparing for all of this for a long time. He didn't tell me. He just did it."

Lisa's dad thought to himself, "Good for you Grant. That's how you have to do it." He kept listening.

"Things are getting bad," Lisa said. "Really bad. Someone attacked us and hurt Cole."

"What! Are you alright?" he asked. He was furious that someone hurt his girl and his grandson.

"We're fine," Lisa said. "But we need to go. Now. I'm going to come by your house with some people to take us out to the cabin. You need to be ready to go by 6:00. I mean ready to go. Everything you'll need for a week or so out at the cabin."

"OK. I'll tell your mom," Lisa's dad said. She was glad her dad answered the phone. It seemed like it would be easier for him to understand the need to go. "Who are these people coming with you?" he asked.

"It's a long story," Lisa said. "But Grant goes shooting with some guys. They're very well armed. He had a plan for them to get us out to the cabin if he couldn't take us himself."

"OK," Lisa's dad said. "We'll be ready by 6:00." He paused. "I am kind of looking forward to being with all of you at the cabin."

"See you then," Lisa said, wanting to get packing. "Bye, Dad."

Now Lisa had to tell the kids. Manda had overheard all of this. When Lisa got off the phone, Manda came running downstairs and jumped up and down. "Yeah! We're going out to the cabin with Dad!" At first Lisa was mad. She was reminded that Grant had left them. But then she was glad, too. "Yes, we'll all be together out there. Now get your stuff together."

"Way ahead of you Mom," Manda said with obvious pride. "I'm pretty much packed. I can help with getting Cole packed."

Cole was glad to see that they were going to the cabin. "No more mean lady? She won't be there?"

Lisa started crying, but they were happy tears this time. "No, honey, no more mean lady. Daddy is out at the cabin and we'll be safe there."

Cole smiled. He wanted to go there so badly. He wanted to throw rocks in the water with his dad. He wanted all the crying and being scared of people to stop. "Dad can tuck me in."

Lisa cried some more. "Yes, Dad can tuck you in."

They spent the next hours feverishly packing. Deciding what to bring and leave behind. That Tahoe held a lot of stuff.

Pow rounded up the guys. Scotty was out on a milk run, so they had to wait for him to get back. "OK, gentlemen," Pow said when Scotty returned, "we're bugging out to Grant's cabin. We're taking his family and his in-laws. They're both in town here. I have all the details."

"What about your neighborhood here?" Wes asked.

"Clay has it under control," Pow said, which was true. Clay and all the vets had this place doing very well; better than most neighborhoods. They wouldn't be leaving the place to the bad guys. Pow thought about Mrs. Nguyen and those like her. She would be in good hands. The neighborhood didn't need the Team. This made leaving much easier.

Pow wasn't worried about his house getting trashed if they left. He rented and so did all the other guys on the Team.

Back in the Cedars, Lisa was done packing. When they had everything, she made sure the stove and faucets were off and the doors locked. It was 5:25. She heard some trucks pulling up. She looked out the front door window and couldn't believe what she saw.

A white civilian Hummer and three pickups. The drivers got out to stand around their vehicles, seeming to be guarding them, and looked like soldiers. Actually, they looked like private military contractors that she'd seen on the news in Iraq and Afghanistan. She felt safe, for the first time in a week.

"OK, get in my car," Lisa said to the kids. She looked around at her house. "Goodbye house," she said. "We'll be back soon." She got in the SUV and hit the garage door opener. "Here we go, kids," she said just like when they were going on a vacation.

Pow came walking up to her in the garage. He didn't have a rifle, but had a pistol on his belt. He had that badge out, too.

"Since you know where you're going," Pow said to Lisa, "you take the lead. We'll follow. We're not in any rush, so don't run any yellow lights with us trying to follow."

Lisa nodded. She was nervous, but trying not to show it. Pow looked in the back seat of the Tahoe, smiled, and waved at Manda and Cole. He pointed to his badge and gave the kids a thumbs up to reassure them everything was OK. Manda and Cole felt safe for the first time in days.

"OK," Pow said, "back out and we'll follow. You all set?"

Lisa nodded again and smiled. She was so thankful for Pow and these other guys. She looked at the clock in the Tahoe. "5:31." She wanted to get out of there. Now.

They slowly left the neighborhood. Len was at the entrance with a gun. Lisa rolled down her window and said, "See you later." Len wondered why she was leaving with the cops in the Hummer and pickups; he had seen their badges.

They headed out on the short drive to Lisa's parents. At an intersection they saw some graffiti in yellow spray paint that said, "There is no gov't." That seemed odd.

Pow remembered that he hadn't told Grant the good news. He tried the voice line; it was down. He typed a text: "Lisa n kids r coming out!! Me and Team 2!! C u round 8 to 9." He hit send. Pow was so proud of himself. He was reuniting a family. And getting the Team out to a safe and well-stocked country location.

Chapter 67

Ten Bucks a Gallon

(May 7)

The guys were following Lisa well. The last trucks would run red lights to stay with the convoy, but no one was exactly handing out tickets. There wasn't a lot of traffic. Lisa was surprised to see most neighborhoods along the way to her parents' had checkpoints, some with armed men. She hadn't been out of the house in several days. Everything had changed. It looked like something out of a movie. She was so glad they were getting out of here.

Her parents' neighborhood didn't have any checkpoint or guard. They drove right in. Are you kidding me? Lisa thought. No guards? Her attitude about armed men guarding neighborhoods had changed 180 degrees during that short ride. She was so glad her parents could come out to a safe place and be with her.

Her dad, Drew, was waiting in their Toyota, with the engine running. It was 5:40. They were early. He got out of the car and yelled for Eileen to hurry up. He looked at the convoy and couldn't believe it. Who were these guys? Did Grant hire some Iraq or Afghanistan vets as mercenaries? Drew felt safe.

Pow got out and introduced himself to Lisa's dad. "Sir, I'm Bill Kung. Everyone calls me 'Pow.'"

"I'm Drew," Lisa's dad said to the unusually tall Korean young man. "Thanks for doing this."

"No problem, sir," Pow said. He pointed to each truck and said, "That's Scotty, Bobby, and Wes, but you can meet them when we get there. I will take the lead." Pow handed Drew a walkie talkie. "This is a handheld CB radio. We all have one, and some spares. Lisa will get one, too."

The CBs were Scotty's idea; he was the "comms guy." They plugged into a magnetic car antenna for great reception, but that wasn't necessary for the short ranges they would be at during the convoy. The CBs were simple to use. Everyone on the Team was very

135

glad Scotty got them. They had given him crap about spending his money on radios when he could have gotten more ammo, but now it was clear he'd made a good decision.

Pow continued with Drew. "If you can't get us on the CB and see trouble or need some help, flash your headlights at me and I'll radio the guys." Drew nodded. Eileen was coming out of the house. She looked hurried and scared. She stared at the trucks and the men in the driveway, looking puzzled. Who were these people? Was all this necessary? They were just going to the cabin. Sure, things on TV looked bad but not in her neighborhood. This all seemed kind of dramatic. Overly dramatic. But she didn't want to argue with Drew, or especially Lisa, in front of Manda and Cole. If Lisa said they needed to leave right now, that's what they would do. Even if it was weird.

Pow came over to Lisa's Tahoe. She rolled down the window. He handed her a CB handheld, and showed her how to use it. He told her about channel 38.

"Mom, I can be the radio person," Manda said. "You need to drive."

"Good idea," Lisa said. Manda was really stepping up in the responsibility department. She had always been fairly responsible, but lately she was acting and sounding like a grown up.

Pow asked Lisa, "Do you have a gun?" Lisa shook her head.

"Yes, I have one," Manda said. "Sorry Mom. Dad taught me how to use it, and I have it safely in my pocket with a holster."

"Manda!" Lisa screamed. "What are you doing with a gun?"

"Mom, look around!" Manda yelled back, which she had never done before to her parents. "What are we doing here? We have a bunch of armed men protecting us because criminals are running around everywhere and there are no police."

Manda paused and continued in a non-yelling voice, "So that's what I'm doing with a gun. Dad said I needed to have one if he had to go."

Lisa could not believe that her daughter had just yelled at her, but she also couldn't argue with that. "OK, but don't take it out of your pocket. And put it away in a locked case when we get to the cabin." Manda nodded.

Pow got a signal from Drew that they were ready. "OK, let's head out. We'll do a radio check." He got into his Hummer. Manda set the channel to 38 and turned up the volume. "Pow here, check?"

"Drew."

"Scotty." It was silent for a while.

"Manda," she said, figuring it was her turn.

"Wes here, check?"

"Bobby."

Pow came back on. "That's the order we'll go in. Me, Drew, Scotty, the Matsons, Wes, and Bobby in the rear. Let's get out of here."

Everyone got into their vehicles. They maneuvered so the vehicles were in the order Pow had given, and then rolled out of the Taylors' neighborhood.

When they got out of the subdivision, Drew came on the CB and said, "Uh, sorry guys, but I need some gas."

Crap. Who bugs out without a full tank of gas?

Pow asked, "How much do you have?"

"About a quarter tank," Drew said. That wouldn't get them there. It would in normal times, but they had to count on traffic jams and going on long detours.

Pow asked, "Is there a gas station on the way toward the freeway?"

"Yes," Drew replied.

"OK, we'll give it a try," Pow said, trying not to let Drew know how pissed he was. "I hope they're open and the line isn't too long." This was going to throw off the whole timetable. They might have to go part of the way in the dark, which meant a gunfight was entirely possible. Damn it.

After a while, they came up to the gas station. The line was pretty long, but moving. Pow came on the CB, "OK, Drew, gas up. Quickly. Anyone else need any?"

Everyone said no. Lisa told Manda how much gas they had. Manda felt like a grown up when she got on the CB and said, "We have three-quarters of a tank. Oh, Manda, that is. I mean the Matson car." She was getting the hang of it.

It took about twenty minutes for Drew to get to the pump. A handwritten cardboard sign on the pump said, "No credit cards. Cash only. Pay inside." Drew motioned to Pow that he was going inside. He had a revolver so he'd be OK, but Eileen was unarmed and in the car. Drew was glad the guys were watching him and Eileen. It was so nice to have these guys around. They were so polite too, saying "Sir" and "Ma'am" all the time. They must be veterans just back from the Middle East.

When Drew got into the gas station, the man behind the counter said, "Gas? Cash only. Ten bucks a gallon."

Drew said, "What? Are you kidding? That's not what the sign

says."

"Sign is wrong," the immigrant man said. "Ten bucks a gallon or nothing at all. You want gas or not?" The cashier was being a dick. He seemed really nervous, probably because he had so much cash in the till and had been dealing with frustrated customers all day. He had a pistol on a holster that was plainly visible. There were several young men that seemed to be his family members standing around and watching every customer.

Drew got out $100 in twenty dollar bills and put it down on the counter.

"Ten gallons on pump four," the cashier said as Drew left. That gas station had always been a pleasant place in the million times Drew had been there before. But not now. It was a mean and dangerous place. Drew didn't want to be there. He wanted to gas up and get the hell out.

He pumped his gas and started to leave. Two women were arguing over something. Drew kept his eyes to himself and got back in the car. Whatever was wrong was between those people, not him. Drew realized that he had never been in a gas station and heard people argue. Ever.

He got in the car and grabbed the CB. "All done. Ten gallons. Ten bucks a gallon. Thanks for waiting, gentlemen. Let's get out of here."

"You paid how much a gallon for this gas?" Eileen asked.

"Dear, this is a stressful enough situation," Drew said as politely as he could. "Please don't treat this like it's the normal world. This isn't normal. We are lucky to get any gas and we're extremely fortunate to have these guys taking us to Lisa's cabin. I need you keeping your eyes open for things on the road. This is not going to be a normal car ride. OK? I let a lot of stuff slide in the past, but not today. I am in charge of getting you to safety. I take my job very seriously. OK?"

Eileen had never heard Drew talk like that. But she was glad he was. He was being a man. She paused. "OK, Drew. Thank you for what you're doing. I can't wait to be with our grandkids." She put her hand on his shoulder. She felt so close to him.

He felt the closeness with her, too. Stronger than he ever had. Her hand on his shoulder was what he needed. He had a hard job ahead. They all did. He needed to know that Eileen was on his side, not complaining about how things were different. Thank God she understood.

Chapter 68

"Trouble!"

(May 7)

The convoy got back into the order they had arrived in and got on the road. It was a short jaunt to the freeway. Luckily, they weren't getting on I-5, which was totally jammed. They were getting on Highway 101, which was a smaller freeway that went from Olympia to the Hood Canal area of Puget Sound. Traffic was very heavy, but not jammed. Pow realized this would be a long ride. It seemed that quite a few people had the same idea they did: bug out toward the water.

Traffic was slow, but it kept moving. This was unlike any ride he'd ever been on. Occasionally, one of the guys would get on the CB and say that everything seemed OK and the others would check in with a similar report. They were going about thirty-five miles an hour, which pleasantly surprised Pow.

They went through the main town out by the cabin, Frederickson. Things seemed like they were in Olympia: people were trying to go out and get food and gas. Everyone looked tense.

The convoy turned off onto the road leading in the direction of Pierce Point. Things still seemed OK. They turned off on another smaller road. It was hugging the beach on the water on the other side of the inlet from the cabin. It was beautiful.

Pow came around a corner and saw a car stopped in the middle of the road, blocking traffic both ways. Two men were waving them down. He yelled into the CB, "Trouble!" and then he realized that he was scaring the Taylors and Matsons. "Everyone stay in their vehicles except the Team. Go!"

The Team had never practiced for this, but they instinctively knew what to do. They slammed on their brakes and tried to park their trucks in the other lane to shield the Taylor and Matson cars from the roadblock. Lisa was just trying to stop her SUV without hitting any cars. She saw the guys jumping out of their trucks with assault rifles. They were using their trucks as shields.

"Get down!" Lisa yelled at Manda and Cole. The CBs were silent for a few seconds, which seemed like an hour.

Bobby came on the CB. "Nothing to the rear. I'm going to the Matson car." Lisa was enormously relieved to hear that. Pretty soon Bobby came running up to their car, motioned for them to stay down, and started pointing his rifle toward the car jamming the road. Bobby would periodically turn around and scan the rear of the convoy.

Wes came running up to the Taylor car. Eileen thought it looked like the Secret Service protecting them, except they weren't in suits. She could not believe how brave these young men were. They didn't even know her; they were just friends of Grant's. Drew pulled out his revolver, not caring if Eileen saw it. That was a concern an hour ago. Now things were entirely different.

Pow came on the CB, "You got the bad guys covered?"

Scotty came on, "Yep."

Pow yelled at the men waving, "Move away. We've got you covered."

The two men with the car blocking the road saw all the trucks with AR-15s pointing out at them. Who were these guys? What the hell?

They put their hands up. "Don't shoot! Don't shoot! Our car is out of gas! Don't shoot!"

To make sure everyone knew what was going on, Pow said on the CB, "They say they're out of gas. Watch the sides and rear." He could hold his AR with one hand and use the radio with the other. He'd practiced.

Pow yelled to the two men in a deep and scary voice, "Walk slowly over to the side. To your left. We will kill you if you fuck around. Understand?" They nodded.

"I got the one on the right," Scotty said into the CB.

"Left," Wes said.

It was quiet for about thirty seconds. Pow wanted to give any of potential accomplices time to show themselves. After it appeared that the two men were alone, Pow said into the radio, "Moving."

"Move," Wes and Scotty said in the radio, nearly simultaneously.

Pow started running toward the car in the middle of the road, scanning right and left with his rifle, hiding behind cover as he went. He didn't want to run toward a situation like this; he would rather wait them out. But they didn't have time to wait. They had to get to the cabin and traffic was backing up behind them. People were honking their horns. It was annoying Pow. He wanted to solve this problem and get going.

Pow made it up to the two men's car. There was no one else there. He looked to see if anyone else was waiting to ambush them. He was glad it was light out and he didn't need to take an hour to do this. Pow didn't see anyone. He looked at the car. Sure enough, there was a gas can sitting there. Maybe they really ran out of gas. They didn't look like dirtbags, but Pow was still very careful.

He pointed his rifle right at the two men and said, "You really out of gas?"

They both nodded, appearing completely terrified. They thought they were being robbed by some...military contractors? That made no sense, which just made the two men more terrified. They had no idea who these guys were.

One of the men said, in a cracking voice, "We were trying to push it to the side. It's in neutral. You can check."

Pow slowly went toward the car and looked. It was in neutral.

"OK," he commanded, "you two slowly come over to your vehicle and keep pushing this thing when I say it's OK." He got on the CB, "They are out of gas. They're going to push it. When I raise my hand, it's OK for them to move. Don't shoot them," Pow said noticing that the men with the stalled car were listening, so he added, "unless you have to."

Pow said to the men, "OK, keep your hands up and slowly come over here to push." Pow put his left hand up. That was the signal for the Team to hold their fire.

The men slowly walked over. When they got to the car, one asked Pow, "Can I get in the car to steer?" The other guy was pushing all alone but they were on flat ground.

Pow nodded. He wanted to help him but caught his politeness impulse and decided to instead scan the area for any potential bad guys. He was getting nervous about the number of cars that were now stopped in both directions. They could have lots of bad guys, or even pissed off guys who might come out and get in the Team's faces. Pow wanted the situation to be simple: just two threats to watch, not people pouring out of their cars. So far no one was. That was probably because it looked like the stalled car was getting off the road.

The man pushed the car. Slowly, it went onto the side of the road. The man pushing put his hands back up. The man steering put his hands out the window for Pow to see.

Pow yelled, "You, in the car, come out and put your hands up."

Once the man did, Pow told both of them, "Stand over there and keep those hands up." They did so.

Pow got on the CB. "It's clear. I'll keep them covered. Everyone else get back in line and we'll get going." By now, the horns were blaring behind them. Feeling agitated, Pow thought about shooting the first car honking its horn, but resisted.

"Where are my manners?" Pow said to the two men with a smile. "You guys need some gas?"

They nodded emphatically.

"We have one gas can," Pow said. He continued to cover the men; just to be on the safe side. Pow held up his AR with his right hand, and used his left hand to work the CB. He said into the CB, "Could one of you round up a hose and the gas can and get these guys some gas?"

"Roger that," Wes said on the CB. He had a short section of garden hose in his truck for siphoning gas. He got the spare gas can from Bobby, drew a gallon of gas from Bobby's truck's tank, and slowly walked up to the car on the side of the road.

Once other people could see the stalled car was off to the side, but traffic still wasn't moving, horns started blaring.

Bobby, the one in the rear, walked up to the cars behind him, raised his AR in the air and yelled, "Shut the fuck up!" The horns stopped. Bobby smiled. That was cool, he thought.

When Wes got up to the two stranded men with the can of gas, they couldn't stop thanking him.

"Let's get this in your car quick," Wes said in his North Carolina accent. "Or we're gonna have to start shootin' people behind us. I've killed enough people today."

The two men froze.

"Just kiddin'," Wes said with a laugh. "Got you."

The two men relaxed. Things were semi-normal. Some nice passersby were helping them. That was normal. For a moment, both Wes and the two stranded men felt like things were normal. That was such a relief.

"Good luck, gentlemen," Wes said as he took the now-empty gas can. He held up the gas can to his head like he was saluting and said, "Now you guys go do something good for someone else down the road, you hear?"

"Yes, sir," they said, which was weird because Wes was younger than them.

Wes got back to his truck and used the hood of it to rest his AR as he covered the car. With his left hand, he got on the CB and told Pow he had them covered. Pow ran to his Hummer. Seeing Wes had the men covered, Bobby and then Scotty got back into their pickups. The time from Wes coming up to the car with the gas can to the Team being back in their vehicles was about one minute.

The convoy started back up.

Lisa had watched this in amazement. She kept expecting some shooting. That's how things always went on TV. She was half-cringing the whole time. But no one got shot. In fact, after she thought about it, these guys in the convoy protecting her and her kids were moving so smoothly that they seemed like guys in the movies.

Lisa was concerned that Cole would be traumatized. He was fine. He just looked out the window. He had complied with all the instructions to get down. He held it together very well. Manda did, too. She never drew her revolver because she knew her mom would get mad.

As the convoy started back down the road, Lisa got the CB from Manda. Lisa said into the radio to everyone, "Well, that's never happened to me before." Her car erupted with nervous laughter from her passengers.

As they were heading down the road again, Lisa thought about the men protecting her family. Did Grant know how to do this stuff? He had been keeping a lot of secrets from her. She smiled. There are good secrets and bad secrets.

Chapter 69

An Absolutely Amazing Sound

(May 7)

Grant woke up. It was evening. He had been asleep most of the day. Even though he was tired, it was a restless sleep.

The night before, while on guard duty, he had finally come to grips with the fact that he'd lost his family. His old life was over. Lisa and the kids hated him. He had "abandoned" his family. No one understood what was happening and what would be happening next.

He checked Manda's cell phone on the night stand. Nothing. No voice mails, no texts. Of course there were no messages. His family wasn't trying to contact him. Don't be stupid. They hate you, he thought.

He heard Chip and Paul out on the deck. It sounded like they were eating dinner. Something smelled good. He got up and went out to be with his new family.

"Morning sunshine," Chip said.

Paul said, "Hey, Grant."

It was a beautiful May evening. They had a plate of BBQ. Paul said, "We're cooking up all the deer meat in our freezer. We might lose power. The power went off for a while today, for about an hour. My mom said the power company has been told to expect rolling blackouts. There's still some bug in the software that routes the power. East Coast had a big power outage today." Paul pointed at the BBQ, "You want some?"

"In a while," Grant said. "I just woke up and I'm still a little groggy." The truth was that he was depressed and had no appetite.

They talked about guard duty. It had been amazingly quiet. They hadn't seen anyone. It seemed that the people who didn't live out there full time weren't coming out, at least not out to the northern end of Pierce Point where they were.

It was good to see Chip and Paul getting along so well. Everyone loved "Uncle Chip."

"I can take guard duty again tonight," Grant said. He had a lot of thinking to do and he wanted to be alone.

"Sounds good," Paul said. "We had you down for tonight, anyway."

Mark and Tammy came over with a plate covered with foil. "More deer steaks if you want 'em," Mark said.

Grant got out a plate. He knew he'd be hungry later and didn't want to insult them by not eating their food.

"Where are John and Mary Anne?" he asked.

"John is on guard duty and Mary Anne is organizing her canning supplies," Tammy said. "We're going to start canning. I haven't done that since I was a kid."

Grant wondered if there were any other disasters that day. "Anyone heard any news?"

Mark said, "Same stuff. It's getting worse. Seattle has full-on looting now. I'm not sure I can trust the news anymore. They're downplaying everything. The TV is just full of politicians telling us how everything is under control."

Mark added, "Hey, the internet is down. I tried to get online for work, just for laughs, since there is no one working now. It's been down all day."

Maybe that's why there hasn't been a text from Lisa, Grant thought. While texts didn't come over the internet, maybe the software for routing them relied on the internet.

Grant felt stupid for even trying to analyze if an internet outage would affect text messages. It was simpler than that, Grant thought. There hadn't been a call or text from Lisa because she hated him. Get over the past. They're gone forever.

Then he heard something absolutely amazing. Car wheels on a gravel road? It almost sounded like Lisa's car.

- End Book Two -

Made in the USA
San Bernardino, CA
14 September 2013